"It's only a dream, it's only a dream . . ."

Diana repeated the words again and again as she paced about the unfamiliar bedroom. "But if it's a dream, why can't I wake up?"

She'd expected to awaken at home in Orlando in the twentieth century. She was supposed to be in her room with its brass bed and wicker furniture. Instead, everything was the same as last night. She was still on Rogue's Cay in the eighteenth century. The little village lay before her, drowsing on the shore in the morning sun. The ancient ship she'd traveled on floated at anchor on the turquoise-blue sea. Her robe lay discarded on the floor. And on the bed . . .

"Oh, no," she cried.

On the bed was her fantasy pirate, Adam Hawke, totally nude.

Madeline Harper's popularity keeps on growing! The writing team's ninth Temptation novel, *Wedding Bell Blues,* hit the Waldenbooks bestseller list in May 1993. And *The Pirate's Woman,* their tenth book for us, is sure to capture even more interest! It's a story about a woman whose fantasy about a dark and handsome pirate comes true when she's thrown back in time. When asked why they chose to write a time-travel book, the two writers explained, ''We love historical novels and wanted to find a way to combine them with contemporary romance.'' When you read about the heroine's voyage into the past, we're sure you'll be glad you went along for the ride!

Books by Madeline Harper

THE PIRATE'S WOMAN
MADELINE HARPER

Harlequin Books

TORONTO • NEW YORK • LONDON
AMSTERDAM • PARIS • SYDNEY • HAMBURG
STOCKHOLM • ATHENS • TOKYO • MILAN
MADRID • WARSAW • BUDAPEST • AUCKLAND

To Susan Sopcek,
for her enthusiasm and support

ISBN 0-373-25576-4

THE PIRATE'S WOMAN

1

"HAPPY NEW YEAR! Have a great time at the party."
Diana Tremont stood on the porch of her shop, smiling brightly and waving goodbye to Alice in Wonderland and the White Rabbit.

As soon as the partygoers got into their car, Diana closed the door of Fantasy Faire and braced herself against it. "Lock the place up," she called out. "I can't deal with one more customer tonight."

Harry Vance popped up from behind the costume-jewelry counter, holding a tray of baubles and smiling broadly to show his vampire fangs. Diana thought her sales manager looked ridiculous dressed as Count Dracula on New Year's Eve, but there weren't many costumes in the shop that would cover his six-foot-four-inch frame.

"You should be celebrating instead of complaining, boss. I'll bet the rentals tonight topped our killer Halloween weekend. This is the best holiday season we've ever had."

"You're probably right, but I'm too tired to celebrate. Let's call it a day—I mean, a night." She stooped and picked up a mask. "How in the world did this get behind the potted hibiscus?"

"Who knows? There's costume jewelry all over the place, too. The customers hit Fantasy Faire like a whirlwind."

Mindy Patterson, Diana's sales assistant, strutted toward the front of the store in her flowing Guinevere costume. "We've all worked hard to make Fantasy Faire a success. Now we're just going to have to pay the price." Mindy struck a dramatic pose and then paused to grab a chocolate from a bowl on the jewelry counter.

Harry tried to pull the candy bowl away from her. "I thought you weren't eating any more chocolate."

"That was before I put this on." Mindy smoothed the flowing skirts of her costume. "It'll hide a few extra pounds." She popped another chocolate into her mouth. "One of the benefits of success."

"It's true," Diana said as she sank into a chair. "After four years of nonstop work, the shop's finally paying off."

Harry took out his fangs and flopped down beside Diana. "But what are you getting out of it?" he asked. "You don't take the time to spend the money you're making."

Mindy nodded ferociously. "Even more important, you don't have time to enjoy yourself." She pulled the wimple from her long red hair and let her hair fall loose around her shoulders.

"Or to respond to you guys," Diana managed.

"Like tonight," Harry continued, unabashed. "You didn't even put on a costume."

"I meant to." Diana was dressed in jeans, a white turtlenecked cotton sweater and sneakers. Her shoulder-length blond hair was pulled back in a ponytail, with wispy ends curling around her face. She looked in one of the beveled mirrors on the wall. "I did put on makeup this morning, but I guess it's all worn off by now."

"I guess so," Mindy agreed, taking out her compact and adding a little blush to her cheeks before running a brush through her hair and replacing the wimple.

Diana glanced at her watch. "Nine o'clock, and no one else is scheduled. We've dressed 'em all tonight, from Cleopatra to Captain Kirk."

"Then let's do it, Diana. Shut this place down."

Harry replaced his fangs and Diana couldn't help thinking what an unusual Dracula he made, with his baby-blue eyes and short spiky blond hair sticking out from behind the mask.

"It's time to party." Harry announced. "We're going to Pleasure Island. Got your wimple on, Mindy?"

Mindy tossed her head. "Yes, milord."

"Want to come, Diana?"

Diana didn't even consider saying yes. The idea of thousands of people packed into the complex of hot, smoke-filled clubs reverberating with loud music gave her a headache. "Nope, I'll pass."

"Not again," Mindy said, chastising her.

"Again? You make me sound as if I've passed up fifty invitations for New Year's. Am I that old?"

"Not *that* old."

"I don't know," Harry disagreed. "Twenty-six is getting up there."

"Spoken from the vast wisdom of your twenty-two years," Diana said with a laugh.

"When did she last go to a party, Mindy?"

"Not Halloween. Not even last New Year's. I can't remember."

"It wasn't that long ago," Diana protested. But she knew it was. Her social life, along with everything else, had taken a back seat to Fantasy Faire. She often worked six days a week, Monday through Saturday, at the shop and then used Sunday to sketch her special designs, which were becoming more and more popular. Her clients knew that if they asked Diana for something original, it would be just that. No one else would show up at a charity ball or fancy gala wearing the same costume. As a result, her following was loyal, intense and demanding.

Harry opened the cash register and began bagging its contents "I'll drop this at the night deposit."

"You're an angel," Diana said.

Outside the shop, there was a squeal of tires as a car pulled into the driveway and came to a stop. The headlights shone through the front door.

"Oh, no. That can't be another customer."

"'Fraid so." Harry moved toward the front of the shop and peered out.

"Don't let him in," Mindy said.

"Shame on you," Harry answered. "This is obviously a desperate case. What do you say, Diana?"

"There's not much left to choose from, but sure, open up," she answered wearily.

"Then I might as well make the most of my time while I'm waiting," Mindy said. "Half the costumes that are left are on the floor. I'll start with the Roman Room."

"You take care of the Ancient World. I'll hang up the Pilgrim, Cowboys and Native-Americans. Keep the customers out of Fantasy and Imagination, Diana. It's a disaster area."

"Call us if you need help," Mindy offered.

Diana heard footsteps on the porch, followed by a demanding, aggressive knock. "Not only late but pushy," she said to herself, fighting back irritation. Heaving a sigh, she unlocked the door, pulled it open and squinted into the night. A man stood between her and the porch light.

"Am I glad you're still open. This must be my lucky night."

The voice was low and mellow, with a lazy sensuality in the inflection that caused an unexpected shiver along Diana's spine. She moved aside and he stepped into the store. As he passed her, Diana caught her breath and held on to the door. She couldn't believe her eyes! It was him!

She stood there, speechless.

Finally he turned back toward her. He was handsome, with thick and wavy dark-brown hair worn long enough to touch his collar in back, eyes that were nearly black and a wicked, sexy grin. Everything about him was so . . . familiar.

"What's the matter?" His forehead creased in a quizzical frown.

"Nothing, I—" Diana's voice trembled slightly, and she broke off in the middle of her answer.

"You seem—I don't know . . ."

He moved closer, looking directly into her eyes. She could feel her skin grow hot under the intensity of his gaze.

"Is the shop closed? Is that it?" he asked.

"No, we're not closed." Diana leaned back against the door, her mind whirling. All her life, it seemed, she'd waited for this moment. Now it was here, and she couldn't believe it.

"Then it must be me," he persisted. "I'm sorry it's late. Maybe I should just leave."

"No, no. It's fine." She struggled to compose herself, willing her heart to slow its frantic beating.

"I promise not to take too much of your time. I'm looking for a costume. Of course, that's obvious, isn't it?"

He wore khaki pants, a dark sport shirt and a brown leather bomber jacket. His tanned skin advertised his love of the outdoors, and when he smiled, as he was doing now, crinkly little laugh lines formed around his eyes.

Diana wished she could stop staring at him. Surely he wondered why she was behaving so strangely. "I'll try to help you," she managed.

"If *you* can't, no one can." He flashed a dazzling, sexy smile. "I have a problem."

He had a problem! Diana shook her head in disbelief. If only he knew the problems he was causing her!

He pulled a crisp white invitation from his jacket pocket. "I've been out of town for a few weeks and I just flew back to Orlando tonight. This was in my mail."

Diana glanced at it and nodded. "It's the Central Florida United Charities Gala."

"How did you know?"

"We supplied most of the costumes for the guests."

"I hope you can dig up one more. I'm on the board of trustees, and if I don't show—"

"The costumes have been terribly picked over, but you're welcome to look. I'll call one of my assistants."

"No, don't do that." He reached toward her, but she moved away so quickly that his hand just brushed her shirt sleeve. "Let me introduce myself. I'm Adam Hawke, and I'm assuming from the sign outside that you are the owner. Diana Tremont."

"Yes." She looked at him and then turned away, trying to regain her composure.

"I feel as if we've met before," he suggested.

Diana was quick to answer. "Oh, no. No, I'm sure we haven't."

"Of course. You're right, Ms. Tremont. If we'd met, I'd certainly remember. And yet—"

Could a man have too much charm? Diana wondered. Everything about him seemed perfect, but that didn't surprise her. He'd always been perfect—in her mind. It was irrational. Impossible. He couldn't be real.

"Let me call my assistants."

"No, I'd rather—"

"Mindy!" she yelled. "Harry! Hey, you two, I need your help. Come and find a costume for Mr. Hawke, something special." She forced a smile. "Mindy and Harry will take care of you. I have other work to do," she managed before she made her escape and scurried up the stairs. Then she stopped on the landing and listened as Mindy and Harry made suggestions.

"What about a toga?" That was Harry.

"It looks like a bedsheet," Mindy answered. "Tacky, tacky. No wonder we didn't get rid of it. Hey, look at this, Mr. Hawke. A knight of the Round Table. You'd look great as Sir Lancelot."

Adam Hawke didn't sound enthusiastic. "Won't it be a little difficult to dance in a suit of armor?"

Harry had another suggestion. "We've got a gorilla costume left. Not a real popular New Year's Eve look, but it might fit...."

Leaving Mr. Hawke to the mercy of her assistants, Diana continued up the stairs, then walked down the hall and into the first room on her right. She flicked on the overhead light and quickly closed the door to her office. She sat down at the table she used as a desk, and opened the center drawer. There was her sketch pad. She took a deep breath and pulled it out. Then she hesitated, almost afraid to open it.

This was absurd, and yet... She got up and walked to the other side of the room, every now and then glancing back at the sketch pad on the table. Mustering all her emotional strength she forced herself to return to the table and open the pad.

Diana's breath caught in her throat.

She hadn't been imagining things. Adam Hawke was the image of the man in her sketch. Her fantasy pirate—the man who'd been a part of her life since she was twelve years old. No wonder he'd scared the hell out of her when he'd walked into Fantasy Faire!

When she'd first begun daydreaming about the handsome pirate, her mother had decided that she'd been watching too much television, too many old movies with Errol Flynn and Burt Lancaster wielding cutlasses and shouting, "Avast, me hearties!"

"You'll grow out of it," she'd told her daughter.

But she hadn't. Diana had just stopped verbalizing her fantasies. They remained, hidden in her subconscious. When she was a teenager, she could hardly wait to go to bed at night and dream of the handsome pirate captain who'd swept her away to sail the seven seas on his ship. She was his captive, his hostage, his princess, and he adored her utterly.

When she'd entered her twenties, Diana had taken a psychology class at the university and learned that her pirate fantasy was simply a longing for freedom, adventure and sexual excitement. It was quite healthy, she'd assured herself, and was nothing to be concerned over.

Often she'd forget about her fantasy lover for months at a time. Then she'd have a dream and there he'd be again, sweeping her off her feet and taking her aboard his ship, to his cabin, where he'd kiss her passionately and make love to her through the night to the gentle roll of the waves.

Diana pulled herself back to the present. She couldn't ignore her fantasy pirate any longer. She turned on the desk lamp and looked closely at the rendering made several months ago. There was no doubt about it. As crazy, irrational, impossible as it seemed—her pirate was Adam Hawke! He gazed back at her, dark and arrogant. The planes of his face were hard, but his lips were provocative and sensual.

There had to be an explanation. Yet there wasn't. She'd never seen Adam Hawke in her life, and yet she'd drawn his image in her sketch book.

"Okay, Diana," she said aloud. "What are you going to do now?" One thing was certain, she couldn't show the sketch to Adam Hawke. But . . . could she show him the costume she'd designed for her pirate?

Diana went to the closet and pulled it out. It was an exact replica, nothing like the pirate costumes in the old movies her mother had laughed at. Over the years, Diana had buried herself in the seventeenth and eighteenth centuries, reading about pirates like Captain Kidd, Blackbeard and Calico Jack. When it had come time to design the costume, she'd carefully studied the library texts on historical clothing. Searching the fabric shops, she'd found just the right materials to make a white shirt with flowing sleeves cuffed with Brussels lace, a wide red silk sash and black knee britches. She'd also come across brocade for the waistcoat, brass buttons and satin ribbon facing. Then she'd taken her sketch to her tailor and had the costume made.

Yet she'd never put it downstairs with the other pirate paraphernalia. She'd always meant to, but for some reason it had remained hanging in her office closet. It was almost as if she'd been waiting for Adam Hawke to come into Fantasy Faire and ask for a pirate costume. Diana would bet every dollar in the cash register that this would fit him perfectly.

Suddenly she made her decision. She was going to march right down the stairs with the costume for Adam Hawke. As soon as her nerves steadied.

DOWNSTAIRS, Adam was wondering what the hell was going on. The two shop assistants were arguing like fishmongers over his costume, while the owner of the shop had fled like a frightened deer the moment he'd arrived.

"How about this?" Mindy asked. "A kilt. Don't you love it?" She held it out for Adam's inspection.

Adam shook his head. "I'm not the kind of guy to wear a skirt. Sorry."

Mindy faced him down, hands on her very ample hips. "Scottish men are very masculine, Mr. Hawke, even when they're wearing 'skirts.' I think you could carry it off."

"No offense," he said. "It's just not my style. I guess I'll have to go with Harry and the gorilla."

"Good choice," Harry said. "Step this way into the dressing room, and we'll get you suited up. The costume looks very authentic, so you'll give the guests a real start when you walk in."

"And you say I'm not going to burn up in that thing?"

"Nope. The suit's got lots of ventilation. I'll admit it's pretty stuffy inside the head part, but once you've made your initial impression, you can take it off."

They were still talking when Diana's voice floated down from the stairway. "Somehow I think Mr. Hawke would make a better pirate than a gorilla."

Adam looked up as she moved from the shadows into the light. He didn't even notice the costume. He saw only Diana, her face glowing. Her deep sea-blue eyes seemed to sparkle, as if she were keeping a secret. Something was going on, and it involved him.

"I think this is the costume Mr. Hawke is looking for."

She walked toward him, and once again Adam was struck by the connection he felt with her. He was sure she'd felt it too—the excitement, even recognition, between them. And how had she responded? By running from him!

Diana handed him the costume. "Harry, see if you can find boots to go with this."

"Ten and a half," Adam said, not taking his eyes off Diana.

"I've never seen that," Mindy said. "Diana, where'd you—"

"We'll talk later, Mindy. Mr. Hawke, the dressing room is that way."

He nodded and went down the hall, his mind still on Diana. He'd been told that her reputation was solid and her style indisputable. That much was apparent in the way she'd renovated the house, making the most of its classic ambience. She'd located in a neighborhood where stately old homes were being turned into trendy shops. There was an aura of class in the wide sidewalks and huge oak trees, but it was still only a few blocks from downtown Orlando. A savvy move on Diana Tremont's part. As a businessman, Adam approved.

"Here're the boots." Harry thrust them through the curtain and interrupted Adam's thoughts.

"Are you ready?"

"Not quite." Adam quickly stripped to his underwear and got into the costume, amazed to find that the shirt and trousers fit perfectly. He tied the red sash around his waist and pulled on the waistcoat. The damn thing seemed tailored just for him.

Moments later, he strode back into the entrance hall with a new swagger in his walk. "You are a genius, Ms. Tremont. This is a perfect costume."

Diana stared at Adam. Here he was, her fantasy pirate, the man she'd dreamed about for all those years. But now he wasn't a dream. He was flesh and blood, wearing the costume she'd designed. The white shirt stretched perfectly across his broad shoulders, and the breeches clung to his muscular calves and thighs. She wanted to reach out and touch him, but she didn't have the nerve. No dream had ever been quite like this.

"What a laugh my friends will have," he went on.

"I should think they'd be more impressed than amused," she managed.

"They won't be laughing at the costume, but at the symbolism," he replied.

"Symbolism?"

"Adam Hawke, pirate of the airways, at your service," he said with a bow. "My rivals gave me the name out of jealousy, and my friends—well, they just like to give me a hard time."

Harry struck himself on the forehead with the palm of his hand. "Of course. You're *that* Adam Hawke! Hawke Airways. I read about you in the business section of the Sunday newspaper a few months ago." Harry turned to Diana and Mindy. "You remember, this guy stole one of Overseas Airlines's biggest Caribbean accounts."

Adam shrugged. "We just offered a better schedule and better terms. And for that," he added innocently, "I get called a pirate. Now does that seem fair?"

Diana was nodding, a relieved smile on her face. "Of course. I must have seen your photo in the newspaper. That explains it! *Subliminal*," she murmured, almost to herself. It was coincidental, not mystical at all. She'd stored Adam Hawke in her memory and drawn his face—and body—on her pirate.

"What?" Adam asked.

"Umm, well... It's a long story," Diana replied. "But it does answer a lot of questions."

"For you, maybe but not for me. I think we should pursue this conversation, Ms. Tremont."

Her answer was decorous and correct. "Perhaps we can talk when you return the costume. Fantasy Faire is open Tuesday and Thursday nights until nine. We serve wine, and the atmosphere is quite festive."

"New Year's Eve is festive, too," he teased. "How about now, tonight? Why don't you come to the gala with me?" He hadn't planned on asking her; the invitation had been totally spontaneous, but after he'd said the words, Adam was very pleased with himself. Then he saw Harry wink at Mindy behind Diana's back and knew he had moral support.

He really wanted to get to know Diana Tremont. Elusive and mysterious at first, then calm and in charge, she'd gone through half a dozen transformations since he'd stepped into the shop. But it was the last transformation that puzzled him—when she'd seen him in the pirate's costume and stared as though seeing a ghost.

What the hell was she all about? Adam decided to persevere. He was used to getting what he wanted, and right now he wanted to spend an evening with this complex woman.

"I don't have a date, and I'm sure you'll know most of the folks there. I think we'd have a good time." He paused before adding, "Unless, of course, you have plans."

"No plans," Harry volunteered quickly.

"It's a great idea," Mindy chimed in. "Go, Diana, go."

"I don't need a cheering squad, Mindy. I'm really exhausted, and after all, Mr. Hawke doesn't even know me—"

"That's the point. I'd like to get to know you. What about it, Ms. Tremont—Diana?"

When Diana hesitated, it was Harry's turn again. "It could be a smart business move. You'll see a lot of your clients there, and they might introduce you to potential customers—"

"I appreciate the offer, Mr. Hawke, but I—"

"If we're going to spend the evening together, I want you to call me 'Adam'."

"Adam," she said softly.

He knew then he was going to win. Her resolve was weakening, and with his two co-conspirators, he had an answer for her every argument.

"Let's find you a costume," Harry offered.

"I didn't say I was going."

"You called him 'Adam,' so of course, you're going," Mindy ordered. "Now what about that dress you designed for Bitsy Jamison? It should be the right time period—early eighteenth century."

"It was too tight in the waist for Bitsy, and it'll be too tight for me."

Adam smiled. She was going.

"Bitsy gained ten pounds between the first fitting and the party. And every pound went to her waist."

"Mindy—"

"Oh, come on, Diana, where's your sense of adventure?" Harry asked.

"I would have thought a woman who'd forged a niche in the business community would be more daring," Adam challenged.

"I'm not the daring type," Diana responded. "I'm the responsible businesslike type who's not given to flights of fancy or . . . or adventures," she said, finishing lamely.

Then Adam did something he'd wanted to do all along. He touched her cheek, gently, lingeringly. It was an intimate gesture and that's what he'd meant for it to be. But it put him off balance, too. Her skin was warm and soft to his touch, her eyes challenging and bright. He realized then that he really *wanted* to spend the evening with Diana, wanted it desperately. He'd rarely been more determined about anything—even winning a new route or coming out on top with one of the major airlines paled in comparison.

"I don't think that's true," he said finally. "I think you have a very adventurous, romantic and highly imaginative side. Otherwise you wouldn't have created Fantasy Faire. You would have called your shop 'Responsible Raiment' or 'Dependable Duds.'"

He saw her lips twitch with laughter as she fought to remain serious.

"So let's do it. Let's live a little fantasy of our own." He kept his eyes fixed on hers, and he could see them soften. In that moment, it seemed as if they were the only two people in the room. "Come on, Cinderella, let's go to the ball," he teased.

"You should probably wear a wig with your costume," she said weakly.

Adam looked at Harry and then Mindy. The conspirators had won. But there was still a point of contention. "No wig," he said.

"Well, maybe we could tie your hair back in a queue. It's almost long enough."

"You can discuss that later," Mindy told her. "Time's wasting, and we have to get you dolled up." She took Diana's arm. "We'll only be a moment, Mr. Hawke."

"Meanwhile," Harry said, "let's head over to the accessories corner. You need a sword—"

"You have swords? Hey, this is better than being a kid in a toy store."

"They're all fake—nasty looking but harmless. We have cutlasses and pistols and scimitars—"

"I'd like a cutlass," Adam said, "and maybe a pistol to stick in my belt. I wonder if I should wear a pirate hat."

"No," Diana called out from the dressing room. "I refuse to go anywhere with a man in one of those silly pirate hats that children wear at birthday parties. They're not at all authentic. The queue will be fine. I'll fix it for you in the car."

"I look forward to that," Adam called after her.

2

"I TOLD YOU this dress would be too tight," Diana complained.

"So suck in," Mindy ordered calmly. "You were the one who designed it. You built the whalebone corset stays into the dress. You—"

"Enough already!" Diana took a deep breath, feeling a little like Scarlett O'Hara dressing for the picnic at Twelve Oaks. "Do the buttons now, Mindy, while I'm still sucked in."

When Mindy obliged, Diana slowly exhaled, and realized that she could almost breathe normally.

"It's spectacular, Diana."

Diana looked in the mirror and nodded. "I have to agree, even if I did design it myself. Peony red for the underdress was the perfect choice."

"And the gilt ribbon along the hem was the perfect touch. I remember thinking when I saw the sketch that all this red and gold and blue brocade was a bit much for the overdress. But it's stunning, and it fits you perfectly. Your waist is tiny and—well, let's say you fill out the top nicely, too."

"Mindy!" Diana tugged at the shoulders of the dress in an attempt to raise the neckline.

"That won't help."

"You're right, but it's much too low." She fluffed up the lace along the décolletage. "There. That's a little better. Isn't it?"

Mindy shook her head. "Nope. But don't worry, Diana, it was the style of the day. Besides, there's nothing you can do about your figure. If you've got it, flaunt it. Now, let's move on to the hair. The curls around your face are very—well, eighteenth century. 'Course this has to go." She tugged on Diana's ponytail.

Diana pulled off the tieback. "I'll use it to hold my pirate's queue."

"*Your* pirate?"

"I'm talking about the character, not the man. Besides, I designed his costume, so naturally I—"

"You're blushing, Diana. I think—"

"Enough, Mindy. Find me a couple of decorative combs for my hair. And I'll need to make a headpiece of some sort. Eighteenth-century ladies never went out with their heads uncovered. Maybe some feathers and a bit of tulle...."

"That should do it. Now, what about jewelry?"

"The fake diamond-and-topaz necklace...."

"I love it! And I'll bring diamond earrings, too—or whatever passes for diamonds at Fantasy Faire."

Within a few minutes, Diana was ready, dressed as a grand lady of the eighteenth century. She looked in the mirror one last time before leaving the dressing room, unable to believe that she was setting off on

New Year's Eve with a stranger, a man she'd sketched but had never met, a man who was dressed as the pirate she'd dreamed about for years.

It was becoming very, very complicated.

They left the shop amid laughter and well wishes from Mindy and Harry. As Adam drove toward the expressway, the strangeness of the situation was very much on Diana's mind.

"I don't usually do this kind of thing. I mean, I never—"

"Run off with pirates?" Adam laughed.

"Go out with men I've only known for half an hour."

"I've given you my credentials," Adam replied, "and there'll be guests at the gala who can vouch for me. But I must admit that I'm not usually this impetuous about my social life, either. It just seemed right for us to go to the party together."

Diana wasn't sure how to respond. She sneaked a sideways glance at him. She couldn't possibly explain how strange this situation really was.

"All I know about you, Adam Hawke, is that you own an airline."

"*And* that your pirate costume fits me perfectly."

"That, too," she admitted. "But since we're going to be together all evening, maybe I should know more."

"My life's an open book, Diana. Fire away."

"Well, let's see.... Did you always want to fly? How did you get started? What did you—"

"One question at a time! Yes, I always wanted to fly. The first time I sat in a cockpit of a friend's single-engine plane, I was hooked."

"I guess being a passenger on a commercial airline isn't the same."

Adam laughed. "Not exactly. If you ever fly with me, you'll see what I mean. There's a sense of freedom, of total abandon, that hits you when you leave the earth behind. 'Course, I was always accused of flying by the seat of my pants, but it seemed so natural to me. The sky was where I belonged, so I thought I might as well make a living up there."

"That makes sense," Diana agreed.

"I moved up to a twin-engine Cessna that I booked for short commuter hops. I did okay, bought two more planes and campaigned for business. Little by little I got it. There's a fleet of eight jets now, and I'm just getting started."

Adam turned toward her, and Diana felt her heart jump at the intensity of his gaze.

"I always know what I want, Diana, and I always get it. That's never going to change."

Once more Diana felt the power of his personality. No wonder she'd agreed to go out with him. He was an irresistible force.

"And how about you, Diana? How did your career get started?"

"I wasn't that single-minded. I kind of fell into costume design after failing as an actress."

"Seems to me you'd be quite an actress. You have the looks and style."

"Thanks, I'm flattered, but I didn't have what counts most—talent. I was lucky, though—classes in costume design were included in the curriculum, and I'd always liked to sketch. It didn't take long for me to get involved."

"Then you graduated, and the trick became how to turn your interests into a career. I know how hard that can be."

"It really was tough at first," Diana admitted. "But my parents lent me the money to lease my first shop. It was about as big as this car. I made all the costumes and then set out creating a need for them. That part's a little embarrassing."

"Tell me about it." He glanced at the clock on the dashboard. "After all, I've known you since nine o'clock. We have no secrets, do we, Diana?" he teased.

If he only knew, Diana thought. If only this pirate realized how many secrets she'd lived with through the years!

"All right, I'll admit that I had a lot of gumption in the early days. I dressed up in my own designs and went to art galleries, restaurants, flea markets. Once I even went to a dog show and handed out Fantasy Faire flyers—dressed like a cat."

Adam threw back his head and laughed. "Bet you got press on that."

"I sure did. I looked like a fool, but it brought in the customers. People were just beginning to dress up extravagantly for Halloween in those days. I guess I was in the right place at the right time. Then I got into the movies."

Adam quirked a dark brow.

"Or my costumes did. One of my friends from the university produced a low-budget film that caught on. I built the costumes for *Swamp Werewolf*. Don't laugh," she cautioned.

"I'm not laughing."

"That got me started. With two major studios in Orlando, I began to pick up more movie jobs. Along with the income from costume rentals, I've done pretty well," she said, trying not to sound immodest. "In addition to Mindy and Harry, I have three seamstresses and a tailor under contract."

"A combination of luck, brains and hard work, I'd say. I imagine you sacrificed a lot."

"I suppose so," she admitted.

"Like your social life?"

"You know too much about me, Adam Hawke," she accused. "I'm not sure I like that."

"You should because we're a lot alike. Confirmed workaholics but with a highly developed love of adventure. Otherwise why would we be heading for a costume ball dressed like an eighteenth-century pirate and his lady?"

"It is kind of crazy," she admitted.

"It would have been crazier not to do it," he argued. "This whole evening has seemed . . . fated."

Adam said the word and waited. Diana studied him suspiciously. "Fated?"

"That's not a line, Diana. It's true. I walked into your shop out of the blue. You had a costume that fit me perfectly and even tied in with my nickname. There was another costume ready and waiting for you. If that isn't fate, what is?"

"Maybe coincidence," she offered.

"There's a Hindu proverb that says, 'Trace coincidence back far enough and it becomes inevitable.' A relationship between us may be inevitable, Diana."

Diana felt a nervous prickle along her spine. She hadn't expected Adam's words to have such a serious undertone.

"So it was fated that we hit it off," he suggested. "Which we did." He'd lightened up and become flirtatious. Diana started to relax. "We didn't start off with a premeditated relationship. We're just winging it. And it's going to be fun."

"I hope so," she agreed. "I haven't had fun—real fun—in a long time. I feel like letting go." She glanced at Adam a little warily, aware that her words sounded more provocative than she intended.

"I feel the same," he said. "It's New Year's Eve and time to let go. But I'm not quite fully costumed yet."

"You look perfect to me." He did, she thought, all six feet plus of him, trim, muscular and sexy. "I mean, you look just like a real pirate."

"What about the hair, Diana? You said I should have a queue."

"Oh, that's right." She rummaged in her bag and handed Adam the tieback.

"You want me to put this on while I'm driving?"

"No, of course not. You can do it when we get to the ship."

"I thought you were going to put it on for me," he challenged.

She had volunteered, Diana remembered. "I'm really not very good with that sort of thing."

"Give it a try." He held out the tieback, and Diana took it.

As he drove, clouds from the east rolled in to blot out the moon and stars. A storm was moving inland from the Atlantic. She moved a little closer to him. "I can't see very well."

"Diana, you don't need to see. Just feel."

He was flirting with her and daring her. Diana took the dare, reached over and touched his hair, smoothing it back with one hand. It was crisp and thick, shiny clean and soft to her touch. As she smoothed his hair down, she felt a delicious shiver that started at her fingertips and raced through her body. She pulled back her hand.

"What's the matter?"

"Nothing," she replied. Diana was letting her imagination run away with her. She reached out again, grabbed a handful of hair and quickly wrapped the tie around it.

"There," Diana said, returning to her side of the car. "One hundred percent pirate." She eyed him appraisingly. "I haven't known many airline CEOs. None in fact. But I would have thought they'd have very short haircuts."

Adam smiled, and even in the darkness, his smile was devastating. "I'm a very different kind of CEO. In fact, I'm a very different kind of guy, Lady Diana. The more we know each other, the more you'll realize that's true."

Diana looked out the window. The cloud-strewn night closed around them, and in the glass she saw her reflection—an eighteenth-century woman dressed for a ball. Beside her was Adam's image—a swashbuckling pirate. The sensation was definitely eerie.

Although they drove along a modern expressway in a luxury car, the reality seemed to fade away, out of existence, as the past enveloped them. Reality and fantasy blurred in a very disturbing way, just as present and past had intermingled. For a moment, Diana felt lost. Then Adam's words pulled her back to the present.

"Here's the turnoff for Cape Canaveral. Adventure—and fantasy—straight ahead."

ADAM WAS IMPRESSED with the *Swan*, an exact replica of an eighteenth-century schooner, which had been restored by a billionaire from Palm Beach at a cost of several million dollars. The owner was willing, if the cause was good enough, to turn the ship over to charitable organizations for their fund-raisers, and United

Charities of Central Florida considered it a real coup to hold their gala on board.

The setting was heightened by the lavish buffet, fine champagne, popular orchestra—and no less by the threatening skies and occasional gusts of wind that added drama to the scene. Adam felt as if he could roam the ship with Diana all evening, but she was spirited away from him.

She'd told him that most of the costumes at the party had come from Fantasy Faire. He'd taken that as a slight exaggeration, but it had turned out to be true. Moreover, the guests who'd rented costumes from her were more than customers; they were friends.

Adam also knew many of the people present. He didn't miss the meaningful looks when he and Diana joined a table for dinner. The looks pleased him. He was proud to be Diana's escort.

Finally he got up from the table and bowed low in front of her. "Will milady favor me with a dance?"

"I'd be delighted, sir."

Adam liked dancing with Diana, liked the feel of her in his arms, the way she fitted against him. He liked the scent of her perfume and the soft womanliness of her curves. He couldn't help fantasizing about Diana Tremont and the evening ahead for them.

Then someone in a cowboy costume cut in and danced her away.

ADAM STOOD AGAINST the polished teak rail, absently sipping champagne and watching as an Aztec warrior cut in on Napoléon and then stepped aside for Superman. Every man in the place, it seemed, wanted to dance with her.

He couldn't blame them. The way she looked in the ball gown took Adam's breath away. The color dazzled him and what he could see of her creamy breasts, pushed upward by the dress, was tempting and provocative. His gaze followed her each time she whirled by.

"Enough of this," Adam said aloud, causing the couple next to him to look up, surprised.

"It's time to claim my lady," he explained, moving toward the dance floor. He lost Diana in the crowd but remained patient. She'd whirl by again. When she did, he caught her eye and she smiled.

Adam made his way through the crowd toward her. There was definitely something going on between them. Was it chemistry, karma, fate? For him Diana was a fascinating package of mystery wrapped in romance, and he wanted to be the man to unwrap her.

He strode up to her, his sword swinging against his leg. He was feeling very piratical and macho. He missed on the first try, then managed to tap Diana's elaborately costumed partner on the shoulder when they swirled by again.

"It's my turn, Casanova," he said.

"Regretfully, I must give you up, milady." Casanova bowed low and with a gesture of farewell disappeared into the swirling throng.

Diana was still giggling as Adam took her hand and headed for the nearest exit.

"Where're we going?"

"Ashore," he called out. "Away from the various sheikhs and sultans who're pursuing my date. Or should I say milady?"

"My goodness, Captain Hawke, you're very dashing tonight, spiriting me away."

"I had to kidnap you to get you to myself." Adam led her along the deck, down the gangplank to the jetty. There they were protected from the gusty wind, and the sound of the orchestra drifted toward them. "This is more like it," Adam said, holding out his arms.

Diana seemed to flow into him. He put both arms around her waist and held her close, moving slowly to the rhythm of the music. "Nice, eh? Our own dance floor."

"More than nice. It's magic, Adam." She looked up at him and smiled. Her face was bright and animated, and she seemed to be free from whatever had bothered her earlier.

"We'll have to do this again—without the costumes. Unless there's someone special in your life who's going to challenge me to a duel."

"There's no one special," she answered immediately. "What about you? I mean, is there anyone—"

"Only the woman in my arms," Adam replied. "I'd like to see you again. What about tomorrow afternoon at about two at the airport? Will you come flying with me?"

Diana's laughter floated over the water. "Sounds great, but where will we go? The Bahamas? Jamaica? Or Rio? I've always wanted to go to Rio, but travel by pirate ship is sooo slow...."

Adam played along. "Dinner in Rio sounds good, but I have a better idea. I've just started flying to a place in the Bahamas called Rogue's Cay. It's a miniature paradise off the beaten track. I think you'd like it." As he held her closer and swayed to the music, Adam realized he was no longer teasing. A few days with Diana Tremont on a tropical island sounded like a great way to begin the new year.

Diana closed her eyes and melted into Adam's arms, snuggling close and giving in to a fantasy about her pirate. She and Adam were flying away to a romantic island, sharing a rum punch, soaking up the sun, swimming in turquoise blue waters, lying together on hot, white sand, making love—

Diana gave a little start at the vividness of her dream and opened her eyes.

"Are you all right?" he asked.

"Fine. Just lost in thought," she answered immediately, afraid he might be able to read her mind—and see her fantasies.

"It's easy to lose yourself in daydreams about the islands," he said. "And who knows? Maybe someday..."

They stood on the jetty in the shadow of the big ship, as the music faded out.

"Maybe we should—"

"Go back?" he said, finishing for her. "The music has stopped, and everyone's getting ready for midnight."

They could hear the raucous laughter, the sound of horns, noisemakers and the premature shouts of "Happy New Year."

"Do you want to join the celebration?" he asked, "or find a quiet place just for us?"

Diana's eyes met his and held. "A place of our own," she said softly.

Adam took Diana's hand, and they walked along the gravel path that led from the jetty to the beach. Just as they reached the shore, the wind grew stronger.

Diana looked up at the sky. "There's a storm coming." The wind intensified, pulling at Adam's loose pirate shirt and billowing the wide sleeves of Diana's dress. She found it exhilarating—not frightening at all.

"You like it," he said.

"Yes." She gazed at him, silhouetted against the sky. She felt lighthearted and giddy. Her fantasies were coming true. Adam wasn't just playing the pirate role. He was the pirate—her pirate.

He'd given her this special, magical night. Everything about him made her feel special. She even felt as if she could tell him about her fantasy pirate, the sketch, the costume. So what if it sounded ridiculous? She was sure he wouldn't laugh at her now.

In the distance the noise grew more raucous. Midnight was only a few minutes away. Adam slipped his arm around her waist. He'd wanted to kiss Diana all night. "I know it's not midnight yet, but practice makes perfect."

His lips grazed hers. She drew back a little, but not far enough to deny him the kiss he so desperately wanted.

He touched her cheek with his fingertips and let his hand drift along her face to her throat. Then he turned her face back toward him and captured her lips. She tasted of champagne. When her mouth opened under his, he tightened his grasp on her.

Adam didn't want the kiss to end. Her breasts were lush and soft against the fabric of his vest. His eighteenth-century breeches were growing uncomfortably tight as his excitement increased and the kiss deepened. There was no doubt in Adam's mind that this moment was meant to be.

He moved his lips a fraction of an inch away from hers so he could speak to her. His voice was hoarse. "Diana, I don't want this night to end. I want—"

Even the burst of thunder and the bright flash of lightning that caused her to jump didn't faze Adam.

The heavens could fall, and he'd still want to do nothing but kiss Diana.

His lips claimed hers again, and this time he explored the soft recesses of her mouth with his tongue. Diana threaded her fingers through his hair, and when her own tongue tentatively touched his, Adam enfolded her in his arms. He wanted more than her kisses; he wanted to make love to her, slowly, passionately, all night long.

Then, with sudden and unexpected ferocity, the storm was upon them. Thunder crashed loudly; lightning illuminated everything around them.

"Damn," Adam said, "we'll have to run for it—"

"Back to the ship?" she asked against his mouth.

"Nope. We're heading for the car. I'm going to kidnap you, Lady Diana, and take you . . ."

His words were lost in a roar of thunder. Then the rain swept through, a squall that threatened to blow itself out within minutes but carried with it a deluge of rain.

Diana suddenly remembered the silk, satin and brocade of their costumes and turned toward the nearest shelter—the low arms of a live oak tree set back from the beach. She began to run. Adam tore through the sand behind her.

"Stay away from the tree—the lightning—" he called out, but his words were lost in the deafening sounds of the storm.

The wind caught her feather-and-tulle headpiece and tossed it into the air. Diana let it go as she grabbed the hem of her dress and tried to keep running. The sand filled her shoes, the rain stained her dress and the wind tore at her hair.

The next flash of lightning was much brighter than the one before, brighter than anything she'd ever seen. Diana stopped in her tracks, awestruck at the tremendous force of nature. Its eerie radiance bathed the world around her in an unearthly white light. In that one flash she saw with perfect clarity the *Swan* bobbing wildly on the sea, the silhouette of the oak tree and Adam, her pirate, shouting against the wind.

Then there was another—final—flash and everything exploded in a fiery red glare. Lightning slammed into the tree, and she threw up her arms to protect herself as a huge branch came crashing down upon her.

3

"Oнhh," Diana moaned as she tried to lift her head.

The room was creaking eerily and spinning like a top. She closed her eyes and willed herself to relax. After a while, she slowly opened one eye. The whirling had stopped, but not the creaking. What was going on? Tentatively Diana opened the other eye and looked around.

She was in a cabin aboard ship, and she had a violent headache. Shakily she touched her head, and felt a knot the size of an egg. A limb from the tree must have broken off and hit her.

What a stupid thing to do, Diana chastised herself. She knew that Florida was the lightning capital of the world, and taking shelter beneath a tree was asking for trouble. She remembered Adam calling out for her to stay away from it, but like a fool she'd raced ahead.

Where was Adam now? Obviously he'd brought her back to this stateroom on the *Swan*. She squinted and looked around. The place certainly was authentically restored, she noticed, from the wooden walls to the oak table and teak desk piled with charts. There was even an oil lamp hanging above the table and a damp, musty smell that seemed reminiscent of another time. She and Adam had glanced into a few staterooms when they'd first boarded, but they'd all been modern versions of the eighteenth century. This room was remarkably restored, even down to the coarse bedclothes on the narrow, built-in bunk. But Diana couldn't appreciate it as she would have liked because of the damned throbbing of her head. It was too bad she'd had to get hit by a tree in order to see the ship's museum room.

Slowly she sat up, only to be overcome by dizziness. She fell back onto the pillow. It seemed as if the entire room were moving. Above the desk, the oil lamp swayed, back and forth, back and forth, mesmerizing her. And the noise—the creaking of the ship's boards—was loud and persistent. She hadn't noticed that during the ball. What was happening?

The storm must still be raging, Diana decided, its harsh wind rocking the boat. She lay back again and tried to relax, but that wasn't possible. On top of her awful headache, there was the strangeness of the room—or cabin, she supposed it was called. The authenticity included unusual brass nautical instruments on the desk. The names sextant and quadrant came to her mind, but she had no idea if that's what the objects were.

There was a greenish glass bottle filled with some kind of dark liquid and two pewter mugs on the table. Great, she thought. Simulated rum, when what she wanted was a glass of water and two aspirin.

Determinedly Diana sat up and attempted to untangle the hair that was matted around her head. Unfortunately her comb and mirror were in her handbag, which, in an attempt to remain true to the period, she'd left in Adam's car. Well, damn the period, she thought. The ball was over, and the twentieth century had returned. With it, she expected aspirin and a hairbrush.

Swinging her feet onto the floor, Diana tried to stand up. It was impossible—not so much because of her headache but because of the movement of the ship. For a moment, she could have sworn the *Swan* was under sail.

"Don't be ridiculous," she scolded herself aloud. The ship was docked—permanently docked. She wasn't going anywhere. But the gala guests had probably gone home long ago.

Yet there was noise from above, voices that seemed to be yelling back and forth to one another. The cleanup crew, she imagined, trying to repair the storm's damage. And somewhere up there, Adam was—she hoped—planning to get them out of here and on the way home.

"Oh, Lord," she said aloud. "I hope he hasn't done something foolish—like calling a doctor or an ambulance." She'd been knocked out only for a few minutes....

Diana stopped in midthought. Or had she? Could it have been hours, even days? No, she told herself—it wasn't possible! If that much time had elapsed, she wouldn't still be on board. She'd be at home—or in the hospital. She looked around, but in this authentic eighteenth-century room, there was no clock. In her authentic eighteenth-century costume, she had no watch. She had no idea how much time had passed.

She had to get out of here and find out what was going on, Diana decided, tentatively attempting to stand up again.

She was halfway to her objective when she heard a key turn in the lock.

"What's going on?" she cried out. "Why was I locked in here?" Diana felt a prickle of unease.

"We always lock up our prisoners," Adam said as he stepped into the room. "Because of your high position, I am allowing you to remain in my cabin. The *captain's* cabin," he repeated for emphasis. "But, do not ever doubt that you *are* my prisoner."

"What high position? What are you talking about?" Diana looked at Adam with astonishment. Why was he talking such gibberish?

The swaying lamp threw his shadow eerily against the wall and made him seem larger than life, and somehow menacing.

"Your games will not work with me, milady."

Diana peered at him through the hazy light of the lantern. His voice sounded strange, and he looked...well, different. It must be her headache and its throbbing pain, Diana told herself. She blinked and looked again. He was still wearing the black trousers and boots, but he'd removed his vest. His shirt was torn and dirty and he appeared to have been in a fight.

No, that was ridiculous. How could he have been fighting? They'd left the gala and gone for a walk on the beach. He must have been injured in the storm, too.

Diana tried again. "Adam, what's happening? I hit my head and—" She rubbed her forehead. "I'm a little confused about things. Is the gala over?" When he didn't reply, she continued, "The party, the ball?"

His lips quirked in a strange, mocking smile that she couldn't understand. "I would say that for you the ball is certainly over—for a while, at least. Can I get something for you, Lady Diana?"

"Lady Diana? Well, I guess that's appropriate for the eighteenth century," she said with a smile that he didn't return. "But since you ask, yes, you can get me an aspirin. Then I'm ready to go home. I'm sorry to have ruined your evening, Adam."

Instead of answering, he merely stared at her. Was this the man who'd kissed her so passionately? It was hard to fathom what had happened to make him seem so cold and distant.

Adam strode to the desk, picked up a chart and spread it on the oak table, seemingly oblivious to her. "Prisoners do not dictate the terms of their imprisonment, not even members of the peerage." He didn't bother to look up as he spoke.

"What's this about me being a prisoner? It's not particularly funny, Adam."

He gave her a cool, dispassionate, almost hostile look. "None of this is for your amusement, I can assure you."

His voice was so harsh, so icy, that for a moment Diana was taken aback. Why was Adam acting so damned weird? Where was the exciting and sexy man she'd been with on the beach?

"Adam, what in the world are you talking about? We were caught in the storm. Something—a branch, I guess—hit me in the head. You brought me here, I suppose, and now it's time for us to go. I'm tired, my head is killing me . . ."

"Yes, the storm presented a problem, but you are here, and you will stay here."

"What?"

"You are my prisoner."

"Adam, for God's sake, this is ridiculous, I—" Suddenly Diana caught on. She understood! They were playing out the game that had begun earlier, when Adam had swept her away from the dance and talked about kidnapping her. Even before that—when they'd left Fantasy Faire dressed like characters from the eighteenth century, a kind of game had gotten under way. Now Adam was taking it a step farther. He was the pirate; she was the pirate's hostage.

"Adam, please, this isn't the time to play games. I've just been hit on the head—"

Adam put his hands on the table and leaned forward, looking straight into her eyes. She cringed under his penetrating gaze. She was surprised at her reaction, but his acting was superb enough to be almost frightening.

"What in the world has gotten into you?" Diana couldn't keep the irritation out of her voice.

He quirked an eyebrow but ignored her question. "You are much calmer now, milady. That is good. At least now you can speak rationally. It is quite a change from the way you came aboard, kicking and screaming. You fought as lustily as your ship's crew when we boarded your frigate. But my men prevailed over yours, as I knew we would."

"What ship's crew? What frigate? I was never kicking and screaming! I don't know what you're talking about. If this is a continuation of your game, I'm not interested. My head hurts, and I don't find it amusing to play the part of your prisoner aboard the *Swan*."

"No longer the *Swan*, your ladyship. When my men and I—shall we say—freed her from her former owners, we renamed her the *Black Hawke*. Fitting, eh?"

"Clever, very clever, Adam. You have all the answers. I'm not quick enough to keep up with you." She stood up and tried to take a step, but a sudden swaying of the ship threw her back onto the bed.

Adam hadn't moved, hadn't even reached out to her when she'd fallen. Diana was obviously on her own. "It must be the storm that's causing all this rocking."

"Hardly, milady. We are under sail, and the seas are high."

"Come on, Adam, enough is enough. The next thing I know you'll be saying, 'Come here, you saucy wench,' and 'Avast, me hearties!'"

He stood up then, to his full height, which was suddenly very impressive, and looked her up and down. Diana felt the heat of his gaze and automatically covered the top of her dress with one hand. She cursed herself for letting Mindy talk her into wearing the low-necked gown that exposed far too much. And yet, when she'd been with Adam before, she'd felt quite comfortable, even appealing, in the costume. But the mood had suddenly changed.

The smile on Adam's face was almost wolfish. "Aye, lady, you *are* a saucy wench, and a lovely one. Far lovelier than I was told by my spies."

Adam was totally into the part. Diana didn't like what was going on—she hadn't been able to get him out of his role, even for a moment. There was no humor in it now, nothing of what she'd seen with Adam before. Everything was different.

"You're making me nervous, Adam," she said flatly. "Let's cut out the game playing and go back to Orlando."

"Orlando?"

"Yes, Adam, Orlando," she insisted. "Now!"

"I do not understand, but it does not matter. We have another destination."

He moved slightly with the sway of the ship, and Diana noticed the power of his shoulders—and how his hand strayed alarmingly close to the shiny sword at his side, which didn't look like a prop from Fantasy Faire.

"You will know about it soon enough," he said.

This time Diana managed to get to her feet, staggering a bit before she crossed the cabin to the porthole and peered out. The boat appeared to be moving, but in the blackness she couldn't be sure. Maybe it was the waves; maybe it was the tide—or maybe the ship was really under sail.

That was ridiculous, Diana told herself. The *Swan* was anchored permanently; there was no way he could have hired a crew to sail it out into the Atlantic. It wasn't possible. And yet . . .

She glanced out the porthole again and had the distinct impression of movement. Dammit! She hadn't signed on for a cruise, but it appeared as though this immovable ship was moving. Was this a dream, a nightmare, or—

"Who hired you, Mr. Hawke? That's what I want to know. This wasn't what you led me to believe—some innocent, last-minute date. All this was arranged. Someone hired you, and I want to know who it was."

Adam walked to his desk, picked up one of the brass instruments and turned it over carefully in his hand, looking past it to Diana. "No man hires me," he said. "I am free as the wind."

Diana threw up her hands in disgust, a gesture somewhat spoiled by the sudden roll of the ship and her loss of balance. "Come on. I hope you didn't write that dialogue yourself. It's so corny."

Adam gave her a puzzled frown.

"Oh, now you're playing dumb—as talented in your actions as your speech, I see. Whoever hired you certainly didn't go through central casting. You're a very special actor."

"Actor?" He put the instrument down on the desk and turned to her with a look of amusement mixed with scorn. "A thespian? Hardly, milady."

Whatever the dialogue, Diana decided, he *was* acting, and doing a very good job. He'd probably gotten a laugh when Diana had told him about her hopes of being an actress.

She couldn't help thinking about their earlier conversation, his intent interest in her past. That high-flown romantic talk about fate and their inevitable meeting was all pretense. Adam Hawke was a faker of the first order, and she'd fallen for him. Even the kiss seemed like a theatrical setup, with the beach, the rolling clouds, the wild wind. Diana tried not to think about how much she'd enjoyed it. She was extremely irritated at herself for being taken in, and she was determined to put him in his place.

"I'd suggest more work with your voice coach," she told him snidely. "Your accent is all wrong. It should have a touch of British—"

"British!" A cold hard look came over his face. "I was born in Maine. I am a colonial, and I speak like a colonial. As for you, British born and bred, why do you speak as if you had never set foot on English soil?" He rested his black boot on the wrought-iron trunk beside his desk and leaned over, arms on his knee. "In fact, Lady Diana, your accent is unlike anything I have ever heard."

"Okay, Adam, I'll play it your way." Diana knew she had no choice; whatever was happening, she would have to go along with it. The sooner the game was over, the sooner she'd get out. "So give me a hint about my role. I'm Lady Diana Tremont, and I'm being held hostage. I wonder why."

"That is none of your affair. Let it suffice that when my conditions are met, you will be released."

Diana smiled. She wasn't as alarmed now that she had the complete picture. In fact, the game they were playing might be amusing, under other circumstances. But with the swaying of the ship, her headache was growing worse. She was quite sure Adam Hawke—if that really was his name—was an actor, not a demented kidnapper. And she could only suppose that Mindy and Harry were the perpetrators. How they'd managed to orchestrate the evening, she wasn't sure, but obviously they'd found her sketch, hatched this elaborate charade and hired this man to play the role of Adam Hawke, past and present.

As irritated as Diana was, she couldn't hide a certain curiosity. "One thing bothers me. Your hair seems longer, and yet that's not possible. I put the tieback on myself, remember? You insisted that I do it. But it looks different. Is it a wig? Or hair extensions?" She reached toward him.

The quick movement of his hand surprised her as he grabbed her wrist and pulled her roughly toward him.

"I do not know your game, Lady Diana, except to confuse me with talk of hair and wigs. I think it best you stay seated."

For a moment, Diana felt a shiver of fear travel up her spine. It wouldn't last. It couldn't last. This was only a game. He was acting, and all she had to do was react. It was that simple.

"I understand the reason behind your outburst, and the cold, steely looks. More like Clint Eastwood than Errol Flynn, actually, but it works."

His only reaction was to hold her more tightly, with a grip like iron around her wrist. As he pulled her to the bed, Diana realized how big and tall he was, and when she fell back, he stood like a giant glowering down at her.

"I said no more of that confusing chatter. Pretending to be a madwoman will not hasten your release."

She tried again to joke him out of the role. "Where in the world did you learn this technique—at the Actors' Studio? You're really immersed in the role, aren't you?"

He grasped her shoulders. "No more prattle, woman!"

Diana pulled away, damned if she'd be intimidated by a hired actor. She noticed the rip in his shirt. "We're going to have to charge you for the shirt because I'll never be able to rent it to anyone else. And this bloodstain—"

"Cease the talk immediately!" He shook her, not too gently. "Your mouth is enough to drive a man into insanity. My patience is growing short, and I have a mind to tie you to this bed."

Diana pulled away. "Don't you even try it! This macho act has gone far enough. I know this is supposed to be a joke, but it's no longer funny. I want—no, I demand—that you take me home. Now."

For an instant, the harsh look on his face softened. "There is spirit underneath all that prattle. I like that. So many of your countrywomen have no spine." He moved away with a mocking little bow. "I shall respect your wishes and not tie you up as long as you behave. But as for releasing you . . . in due time."

Diana sighed. It was hopeless. The man wasn't going to give up his character no matter what she did. "Whatever you say, Mr. Hawke. I'm too tired to fight you any more."

"*Captain* Hawke, if you please. Let me offer you something. Cheese, bread? The fare aboard the *Black Hawke* is simple but filling."

"No, I ate at the gala. What I really need is aspirin for this headache." She touched the throbbing bump on her head.

"This is the second time you mentioned 'aspirin.' Is that a potion of some kind?"

Diana sighed again and leaned back against the pillows. "Oh, you're good. Really good," she said wearily. "Potion. Very quick on the uptake."

"Quick to know when I am being mocked for offering hospitality." His face darkened.

Diana shook her head. Even in this game, he was certainly a mercurial type. "Sorry," she apologized. "I keep forgetting the script."

He reached for the bottle on the table. "This is claret. Very fine. It's been known to clear the head after one sip." He poured some into a pewter mug and held it out to her.

Diana started to refuse but gave in. It was easier to go along with him than to argue. "All right, sure. I haven't had a fine claret in years. Never, in fact."

She took a sip. "It's very strong. But good," she admitted, taking another taste.

"Does it help your head? Try a little more."

She sipped again. "I must say, it warms me thoroughly."

A knowing smile curved his lips. "I am glad you find it pleasing."

Diana drained the mug and handed it back to him. "It is helping my head. There's a numbing effect, actually."

"Good. You will rest." He stood back. "I will leave you, then, to go above decks and chart our course."

Diana nodded. That was a good sign, too. Obviously the cruise to nowhere had lasted long enough. They were finally heading back to port, where no doubt her friends were waiting to share the joke. Or maybe they were already on board, ready to burst into the cabin.

"You do that, Hawke, and tell the crew to step on it." She giggled and covered her mouth. The claret was stronger than she had expected, and the numbing feeling was more pronounced.

She heard him turn the key in the lock. Dammit, that was irritating. Who did he think he was, locking her in? What nerve the man had.

Diana went to the door and turned the knob. It wouldn't open. She kicked at it, which only served to make her dizzier. She shouldn't have had the claret. Grabbing at the door handle, she recovered her balance and then, slowly, managed to make her way back to the bed.

Her head was whirling again, and the room was spinning, whether from the waves or her own dizziness, Diana no longer knew. There was a thick, heady taste in her mouth, and she felt as though her limbs were made of rubber. This was worse than before. She was woozy... sleepy, so sleepy—

"Oh, no!" she shouted, stunned by the sudden realization. "The fool has drugged me!" Her words were slurred and heavy. Everything was out of control. This had gone too far, she thought. She was going to give Mindy and Harry a piece of her mind when she got home. She was going to...

Before Diana could finish her thought, she slipped into the deep abyss of sleep.

WHEN SHE REGAINED consciousness, Diana opened her eyes to blinding daylight, shafting down from high above. Looking upward, she saw that the room vaulted to a towering height, where arched slates were windowed to reveal a bright blue sky.

She lay on the narrow bed, mesmerized. Apparently the cabin was in the ship's bow, below the lofty masthead, which she'd seen when she and Adam had arrived at the party.

Adam. Where was he, and *who* was he?

As if in answer to her question, she heard his voice bellowing at her.

"Lady Diana, rouse yourself." He knocked loudly on the heavy oak door.

It was Adam's voice, but was it the charming man who'd brought her to the party, or the captain, who'd locked her in—and drugged her?

That memory set Diana's head reeling. She'd been imprisoned in a room on the *Swan*—the captain's cabin, which she hadn't even seen during their party tour—and then drugged by the man who seemed to be Adam Hawke—but wasn't.

What a fool she'd been, Diana berated herself, to go out on New Year's Eve with a perfect stranger in the first place. And now, she was involved in—God knows what, maybe some kind of criminal scheme, for all she knew.

A key rattled in the lock. Diana cringed and closed her eyes in a vain attempt to pretend sleep and somehow avoid him—or force him to go away and send someone else to explain what was going on.

No such luck, she realized as the door was flung open.

"It is time to disembark," he ordered.

Behind still-closed eyes, she wished for the old Adam Hawke, a stranger, yes, but one who would probably laugh, take her hand and tell her it was all a joke.

She opened her eyes. It was Adam, but he didn't smile, nor did he take her hand. Instead he frowned down at her, his eyes narrowed. He was still dressed in the pirate outfit, but in the bright light of day he looked less like a man in costume and more like—she might as well admit it—like a real pirate. Dangerous. Big, powerful and dangerous.

His hair was tousled and windblown; the shadow of a beard darkened his face. "Damn," Diana whispered under her breath. He was still playing the role of Captain Adam Hawke, rogue pirate of the Spanish main.

"Dear Lord," she prayed softly, "make it all go away."

Ignoring her plea, Adam grabbed her arm, none too gently, and pulled her to a sitting position.

"I'm taking you ashore."

"We're going back to Orlando? Thank heavens, Adam! I don't need to go to a doctor or anything." She touched the bump on her head. "It's gone down considerably. Not even very sore," she assured him. "If you could just drive me home—or even back to the shop. I know it's New Year's Day, but I probably should drop by just to see—"

Diana stopped short, aware that she'd been babbling. She was more acutely aware that he was still holding on to her arm, forcibly, staring down at her with a look of total incomprehension. It wasn't working, this game of hers to make him—and herself—believe that everything was all right. Not when everything was very, very wrong.

"Your home is far away from this place, milady. I am taking you to *my* house. There, whatever physical problems you complain of will be looked after, and you will be made comfortable until we hear from your godfather about the ransom."

"What in the world are you talking about?" She tried to pull away from him, but he held fast. "I don't have a godfather." This time she pulled harder and succeeded in extricating herself from his grasp. "And keep your hands off me, Adam."

"Pardon, your ladyship." He gave a mocking little bow. "But if you would do as you are told—"

"Why should I do what *you* tell me? Who are you, anyway, except some actor paid to trick me or kidnap me or whatever the hell you're trying to do."

"Not exactly kidnapping—"

"Don't give me any more of that ransom talk. I'm very tired, and I want to get out of here."

She looked up at him and felt a sudden chill. His lips tightened, his eyes clouded over and she could see a muscle jumping in his cheek.

"You have the most unladylike habit of interrupting me, madam," he said. "If you continue to do so I may lose my temper."

Diana decided immediately that she'd best avoid that situation, but she couldn't avoid his presence. His body filled the space before her, and the powerful muscles of his shoulders and arms seemed massive from where she sat on the narrow bunk.

"Sorry." Diana tried another tactic. Assuming all the dignity she could manage, she pushed the hair away from her face and made an attempt to smooth out the wrinkles in her dress. "Maybe you should explain who this godfather of mine is."

"Everyone on both sides of the Atlantic knows Sir Winston Grenville, deputy governor of Maine. You play the innocent well, milady."

"And you play your macho pirate role equally well, Captain Hawke," Diana said, complimenting him and suddenly regaining her prior boldness. "Even in your macho attempts to frighten. And you seem to be as much in character today as you were last night. So I'll attempt to play along with you. Let's say Grenville is my godfather and has the big bucks to pay you if you let me go. Then what will—"

"Enough questions, lady. You know as much as you need to. At this time, we are vacating the ship."

With the little bow she was beginning to despise, he stepped aside.

"After you, milady."

When Diana stood up, the wooziness hit her again.

"Whoa," she said, reaching out and grabbing his arm. "What was in that wine? I know you drugged me—"

"Silence," he ordered impatiently. "I am leaving the ship now, and you are going with me."

"I'm not sure I can walk." Diana still held his arm, her fingers grasping muscles that were as hard and unyielding as stone. Whatever his ruse, there was something substantial about him, and she wasn't inclined to let go. But she wasn't inclined to move, either, even if she could.

Faced with the idea of leaving the ship, she preferred to stay where she was; the cabin was familiar, even safe in a strange kind of way. She couldn't imagine what lay outside. Somehow she knew it wasn't going to be the Florida coast.

Still holding on to him, Diana took a wavering step toward the porthole and peered out. What she saw amazed her.

"Where are we?"

"That, madam, is Rogue's Cay in the Bahama Islands."

"Rogue's Cay! Oh, Adam, it's all right, isn't it? That was your airline's newest destination, the run you liked to make yourself. Remember, you told me all about it...."

"More of your mad babble" was his only response. "This is my home, nothing more."

As he looked out across the expanse of clear turquoise water, Diana followed his gaze and realized that she was not seeing a resort town but an eighteenth-century village, tucked against the side of the hill above an expanse of white beach. It was picture postcard perfect. Too perfect to be real. "Oh, they've built a movie set on the beach," she said. "What fun!"

But it was more than fun. A movie set meant actors, a crew, other people who would return her to reality. It meant a chance to get away from the obsessive and occasionally frightening man who called himself Adam Hawke.

But why was she being brought to a set in the Bahamas? On an ancient ship, of all things. If they wanted her costume advice, they didn't have to kidnap her! Diana tried to think logically, but her mind was too fuzzy to concentrate. She'd find out soon enough what was going on.

"Come, milady. It is time."

Diana tried to take another step, but once again the room was whirling disturbingly. As much as she hated to ask Adam for anything, she didn't think she could make it without his assistance.

"I'm still feeling kind of light-headed," she admitted. "Dizzy, you know, from the bump on my head and the drugged wine . . . so if you could let me lean on you."

"Certainly, your ladyship." Again he bowed from the waist and extended his arm.

4

DIANA FOLLOWED Adam onto the deck, shielding her eyes with her hand. "Wow!" she exclaimed. "The combination of that sun and my hangover—"

"Hangover?" he repeated slowly. "If a man is hung once, that is usually enough."

Diana couldn't keep from laughing. In the real world, Adam probably had a pretty good sense of humor. "All right, stop showing off. I'll admit you're more clever than I. Obviously you know that the word 'hangover' wasn't in the language at the time we're supposed to be in. All I can do is talk like a regular person, but I'll try to throw in a couple of eighteenth-century words now and then—if I can think of any."

He looked down at her quizzically.

"Oh, for heaven's sake, Adam, loosen up. Your insistence on acting the part of ship's captain is becoming irritating. So let's get this show on the road. You want to go to your house, and I want to go to the village and find someone who can get me the hell out of this mess."

"Your wish, my ladyship, is my command, but I must admit confusion at some words in your vocabulary—and surprise at the coarseness of others."

"Try being real, Adam. I'm not in the mood for any more of this ridiculous eighteenth-century nonsense, and I'm not—"

Before she could get out the rest of her sentence, Adam scooped her into his arms, tossed her over one shoulder and headed for the railing of the ship.

"Put me down this minute," she cried, kicking and beating on him with her fists.

"If I did that, you would continue that confounded babbling, and we would never get off the ship. There is only one way to handle a woman like you."

Adam climbed onto the railing and started down the rope ladder to a small boat bobbing on the water below. Diana fought to keep her dress from flying over her head, much to the delight of the men waiting below.

When he stepped into the boat, Adam dumped Diana unceremoniously onto the wooden seat and settled himself beside her.

She sat up straight, with as much dignity as possible under the circumstances. "Adam, I simply won't allow this—"

Ignoring her, he shouted, "To shore, mates. I have had enough of the bloody sea for a while. What about you, Russell?"

"You mought say I'd agree. And if I durst, Cap'n, I'll stop for a bit of grog at the Blood and Bones."

"That sounds good to me, mate."

While the two men carried on a dialogue that sounded as though it came from the pages of a movie script, and a bad one at that, Diana observed the one called Russell, obviously a bit player, but a very convincing one. He was years older than Adam, with straggling gray hair, an ill-kempt beard and the bluest, brightest eyes she'd ever seen. He and his companion pulled on the oars, and the little boat skimmed across the water.

They were dressed very authentically; Diana couldn't have designed better costumes herself. Russell's pants, which had once been white, were dingy, loose fitting and cut off just below the knees. The belt was wide, with a brass buckle in need of polishing. Brass buttons decorated his short blue jacket, and he wore a brace of pistols across his chest. A dirty red bandanna and a gold loop earring completed the outfit.

"Your costume is very good, Mr.—Mr.—"

"Russell Karlen, at your service, your ladyship, and as to me clothes, I think I'll be burnin' them after this trip. No matter how much lye and ashes me woman puts in her soap, there's smells in these here garmints that most would be desirous to avoid."

"You could best use that soap on your own hide, Russell," Adam joked. "He is the best quartermaster on the high seas," he told Diana, "but not much of a fancy man, now are you, mate?"

Russell laughed, showing a mouth of rotting brown teeth. "No, sirree, Cap'n. I leave the preenin' to you."

"Very well done," Diana said, complimenting him. "I imagine that's what passes for repartee among the pirate set." She was feeling more relaxed as they approached the shore. There were people, movement, flurries of activity. The set included a tavern and shops of a small port town. A man lazed in a hammock, another pushed a cart and several women cooked over a bonfire. In the distance a dog barked, and Diana even heard the bray of a donkey.

It was all very reassuring, even though she didn't see the cameras. But she knew they were there. Cameras and cables, electricity and phones, caterers, trailers for the cast and crew—all the amenities of a movie set. She looked up, searching the sky for airplanes. There must be a landing strip nearby—and a way out for Diana.

When the boat reached shore, the crewmen jumped out and pulled them onto the wide beach. Adam followed, reaching down and scooping Diana up and then setting her firmly on the beach. She didn't object this time, although she could have gotten out quite easily on her own. With freedom a step away, there was no reason to antagonize the mercurial captain.

As they walked across the sand toward the little village, a crowd gathered to welcome Adam Hawke. The villagers were all in costume, perfect in every detail.

"Incredible," she murmured to Adam. "I'm really impressed. Can't wait to meet the costume designer, or the set designer, for that matter. They've built an entire village from another century. It's wonderful."

"As usual, Lady Diana, I have no idea what you are babbling about, but I am delighted that for once you are pleased. However, we have no time to stop in the village today. My house is up there, on the cliff above. That is our destination."

Diana looked at the house in the distance. Topped by a red tiled roof, it gleamed white in the afternoon sun. Heavy wrought-iron grills guarded the doors and windows, and a winding path separated the house from the rest of the village. It was isolated, a prison.

"Uh, weren't you stopping at the tavern? What was it? The Blood and Guts?"

"Blood and Bones, and I will leave that to Russell for the nonce. No doubt, I will join him and the others there later."

"No doubt," Diana repeated. "But not now?"

"Not now. Now we are going to my house." He put his hand firmly under her elbow and directed her up the wooden steps that led from the beach to the cobbled street.

As they turned toward the path to his house, Diana balked.

"Sorry, *Captain* Hawke," she said, using his name sarcastically, "but this is as far as I go."

Stepping away from him, she cupped her hands around her mouth. "Hey, someone, anyone! This is a great set you've got here, but I'm Diana Tremont from Orlando, and I'm not part of this damned pirate movie."

A crowd began to gather and listen as she continued. "I need your help to get out of here and away from this lunatic in a pirate suit."

The hulking men and rough women stood silently, staring.

"I need a phone," Diana told them. "Can one of you extras give me some help? Tell me where the director... Hey, I'm serious...."

Finally someone called out, "Aye, Captain, I heard tell she was a handful, but I believe she's gone daft on you."

Diana attempted a break toward the crowd. They were her only chance. Surely one of them would take pity on her and escort her to a mobile trailer where she could use the phone...

After two steps, she was rudely pulled back. With one arm around her waist, Adam held her firmly against his body.

"No more of your deceits," he ordered. "You are coming with me."

"The hell you say! I played along with you while we were alone, but not here, not with witnesses. This charade is over. You aren't Captain Hawke, I'm not Lady Diana and I'm not going anywhere with you." She tried to pull away but only succeeded in twisting and turning in his arms until she and Adam were face-to-face.

Looking down at Diana with steely black eyes, Adam gave her an angry shake. "You do not understand, do you, woman? This is my island—these are my people. All the citizens in Rogue's Cay do what I tell them. You are my prisoner, and you, above all, will obey me."

He turned, and for a moment Diana expected him to fling her over his shoulder again.

But he didn't. He simply held firmly to her arm and pulled her after him.

She tried to dig in with her heels, but it was hopeless; if she didn't jog along beside him, she'd be dragged behind, like a sack of flour. She had no choice but to try to keep up. But she still had her voice; she could still yell.

"Help me, someone. I'm being abducted by a maniac. Call the governor! Call the president! Better yet," she yelled, "call Fantasy Faire in Orlando. It's okay—you can reverse the charges. Tell whoever answers where I am...."

She looked back over her shoulder. The crowed was still there, jeering, laughing and pointing as they enjoyed the spectacle of her being manhandled by this madman in a pirate costume.

Out of shouting range of the crowd, Diana began yelling at Adam. "You've gone too far this time. I know there's a film crew around here. They'll get me out of this."

Breathless, she finally gave up as he continued to pull her along at an ever-increasing pace.

And as the village receded in the distance, she also gave up hope. Despite her brave words, there was no film crew on Rogue's Cay. There was no one but Adam Hawke and his crowd of followers.

WHEN THEY NEARED the house, she regained her momentum and began screaming again, this time flailing out at him. But her blows fell short of their mark as he quickened his steps. Summoning all her energy, Diana caught up with him. Running alongside, at the same pace, she struck a solid blow on his shoulder with her fists. Surprised, he turned toward her and she dug her nails into his cheek.

"She devil," he spit, shaking her off but not loosening his hold on her arm. "I was a fool for not tying you up. I will not make that mistake again."

Regardless of the threat, Diana had already ceased her struggles. The heat, the rugged climb and the strangeness of the situation were having their effect on her. Feeling giddy and sick to her stomach, she was actually relieved when they reached Adam's house.

The cool darkness of the entranceway was a delicious contrast to the fierce sun outside. But before Diana had a chance to take in her surroundings, Adam crossed the foyer, pulling her along, and climbed the wide stairway to the landing above. Stopping at the first room, he kicked open the door and pushed Diana onto the bed.

"Now," he said, "shall I tie you to the bedpost?"

"No, please," Diana begged. "I won't try to get away."

"Your getting away is not my worry." He rubbed the red streaks on his face.

"I won't do that again—I promise. I won't touch you. But you are not to touch me, either."

He laughed down at her. "Do you presume to give me orders in my own home, milady?"

"Yes, I do," she boldly replied. "I'm not accustomed to being manhandled."

"Manhandled? What sort of word is that?"

"Oh, for God's sake, Adam, you know exactly what I'm talking about. This charade is ridiculous—"

He held up his hand. "No more! Every time I let you speak one word it becomes many words. Endless words. You never stop."

He turned back to the door and flung it open. "Mathilde," he bellowed. Then he said to Diana, "I will get the woman up here to assist you, and you can assault her with your endless chatter. Mathilde," he called out again, "where are you, woman?"

The house was silent.

"Damned crone." He pulled aside a screen in a corner of the large room. "At least she has prepared a bath for you. She is lurking about somewhere, spying on us, I'll warrant. I will find her and send her up with your supper."

Diana struggled to a sitting position. "You're going to leave me here? Walk out and send some old woman into my room? Damn you, Adam Hawke, you can't do that."

Adam pulled open the door of a tall wardrobe and selected a brightly colored silk robe, which he tossed across a chair. "I do not take orders from anyone in my house as I have told you before. Certainly not from a hostage, a hellcat with nails like claws and a tongue as loose as the lowliest sailor." He crossed to the door. "Until later, milady. Enjoy your bath," he added with a smirk.

Diana pulled off one shoe and flung it wildly across the room. It hit the door just as he closed it and bounced harmlessly back into the room. "Bastard! Lying, cheating son of a—"

She stopped herself and fell back on the bed. "Good Lord, I do sound like a foulmouthed sailor! Well, why not? Thrown in the middle of such madness, anyone would be swearing," she told herself.

Such madness. Such unexplainable madness. Just the thought of it set her head reeling and sent shooting pains down her back. She rubbed the muscles in her neck, but nothing could stop the pounding pain— or the confusing thoughts that careered wildly about in her brain.

Something really weird was going on. She no longer believed Adam had been hired by Mindy or Harry, and she knew for certain there wasn't a movie crew on Rogue's Cay. Even as she was being dragged up the hill, she'd had a chance to search for the obvious signs—booms, fill lights, cameras, cables and wires.

She'd been on enough film sets to know what to look for. And there was nothing here at all.

A theme park! That idea invaded her mind but was quickly dismissed. She hadn't seen any parking lots or ticket booths or tourists. Diana's head reeled. What was the explanation?

Just then the door creaked open and a small form, swaddled in scarves and shawls, stepped into the room. "You be the one," she muttered threateningly.

Diana felt a flesh-crawling shudder pass over her. "No!" she cried. She wanted to run, but there was no way out. The crone blocked the doorway. Panicked, Diana stepped behind the screen. "Please, leave me alone."

"I be bringin' ye vittles."

"I don't want food. I want to get away."

There was no response, but the woman remained standing at the doorway, her snarled hands holding a plate of food.

"Please, will you help me get away?"

A cackle emerged from the woman's thin lips before she turned away, pulling the door closed after her.

"Okay, I get the picture," Diana said to herself. "I'm on my own."

She stepped from behind the screen, noticing for the first time that it was painted with a bright Chinese scene. She'd hardly had the opportunity to appreciate the amenities in the room. But she certainly planned to fully enjoy the bath.

She began to peel off the absurd costume that had gotten her into this mess. She pulled at the material and finally managed to rid herself of the wrinkled, rumpled ball gown, pitying the poor women of past ages, who'd spent so much of their lives trussed up like Thanksgiving turkeys.

She stepped out of the pantalettes and chemise and eased herself into the wooden bathing tub. The water, although no longer steaming hot, was delightfully warm and soothing, and slowly Diana felt her rigid muscles relax, and her tension drain away.

She was tired, more tired than she'd ever been in her life. Even though she felt dirty and grimy, she barely had the strength to squeeze out the big soft sponge and begin to wash.

She leaned back and watched the droplets of water run down her arm; she knew it was her arm, and yet there was a strange disassociation. She was Diana, but not Diana. How could Diana Tremont, successful businesswoman of Orlando, Florida, be in Rogue's Cay, dragged up a hillside, flung onto a four-poster and then ordered into this antiquated tub by a pirate she had dreamed up?

"'Curioser and curioser,'" she quoted, wondering if this was how Alice had felt when she'd gone through the looking glass.

Sinking lower into the tub, she felt the water envelop her shoulders. Languidly she sank even farther down until the water lapped at her chin. As she relaxed, the tension was drawn out of her body. She closed her eyes and managed to forget everything.

Floating in a dream world, Diana stayed in the tub until long after the water had cooled. Then, reluctantly, she stepped out, dried herself slowly and slipped on the silk robe. The material was luxurious and sensual against her damp skin. Her limbs felt heavy with languor as she slowly moved across the room to the window and looked out on the bright Caribbean, awash with the golds and lavenders and reds of the setting sun.

Diana was relaxed now, warm and content for the moment and very tired. She was turning toward the bed, when something caught her eye, a figure near the house.

In the waning shadows, she recognized Adam. He was walking toward the village. He'd changed from the pirate outfit into a white shirt with flowing sleeves, tight black breeches and shiny tall boots. He strode purposefully and forcefully, his shoulders broad and strong. Even in the dusk, she could see the muscles rippling beneath his shirt. His back was broad and straight, and his rear end was something to contemplate. Diana allowed herself to do just that, nodding with approval. It was definitely a backside worth staring at, and she didn't try to avoid the wave of sexual excitement that overcame her.

His bottom was compact, firm and hard. He had the buns of a dancer, she thought with a smile, imagining what the macho ship's captain would have to say about that. Diana had always wondered what pirates wore under those tight-fitting breeches, and even as a designer, she'd never found the answer to that question. Another question she couldn't answer, another one that made her feel light-headed and giddy.

Weaving slightly, Diana made her way to the bed and pulled back the heavy coverlet. The sheets were white and clean and emitted a fragrance that reminded her of fields of wildflowers.

She climbed up onto the bed and collapsed. A cool breeze wafted across her body, bringing with it another fragrance, the scent of the sea. She'd stopped trying to think. It was impossible to marshal her thoughts in any coherent way without ending up with a violent headache.

So she just let herself sink into the pillows, and allowed her mind to wander.

As soon as she stopped trying to find answers, they began to come to her, floating like white puffy clouds, drifting across the room. She could almost watch them moving, and in the clouds she saw the answer clearly: *nothing seemed real because it wasn't real*. She was asleep, and this was her dream, her fantasy!

Diana smiled softly to herself and all the stress faded away. She was asleep in Orlando in her own bed, and she was dreaming all this. Her subconscious was simply playing with what might have been. More than two days had passed, it seemed, but she also knew that in dreams such long periods of time were often only minutes, seconds, of reality.

Diana sighed with relief and closed her eyes. She had nothing to worry about. Adam Hawke, the airline king, had been transformed into the fantasy pirate who'd swept her away to his secret hideaway, as he'd so often done in her dreams before.

This time the dream was more intense than ever, but she assumed it had been prompted by her visit aboard the *Swan*. Maybe when the limb had hit her on the head she'd experienced a temporary amnesia that had caused her to forget going home. But of course she *was* at home—in her own bed—and she was dreaming of her pirate lover as she had done many times before. Diana sighed with relief.

When she woke up in the morning, her life would be back to normal. Rogue's Cay, the *Black Hawke*... all figments of her imagination.

"Everything's so simple once you know the answer," she murmured into the pillow. Hadn't Adam told her that she was a woman of imagination? "Don't fight it," she told herself. "Just relax and enjoy it. Just let go."

Diana sighed with relief and sank deeper into the feather mattress. The silken robe caressed her breasts and thighs and felt wonderfully sensuous and exotic against her skin. Almost like a man's hands, a lover's hands... Adam's hands.

Her lips curved in a smile. Why not? Why not indulge in a little more fantasy? The real Adam had kissed her, and she'd given herself to that kiss. The fantasy Adam had been intimate in a way; at least, there was a kind of spark between her and her pirate. Why not take it a step farther and give herself over to the eroticism that could be the best part of her fantasy?

In her earlier fantasies, there had always been the hint of something sexual, and yet upon waking she'd never been able to recapture it. Perhaps this time . . .

Diana drifted away on a wave of warmth and sensuality as she imagined Adam touching her in private, secret places. Now, if he would just come back, come into her room and play out the fantasy for her. . . .

THE NEXT THING Diana knew, he was standing by the bed, gazing down at her. The moon cast a shadow across his face, highlighting the hollows beneath his high cheekbones. Adam, Diana thought sleepily, but which Adam?

It really didn't matter, she decided. Here in the depths of her dream, she was imagining her phantom lover beside her bed. She reached out and laid her hand on his thigh. She felt his reaction to her touch, an involuntary tensing of his muscles. But he didn't move away. Of course he wouldn't. Not in her fantasy!

"Milady," he said thoughtfully. "I came to see that all is well."

"Oh, all is very, very well, my captain." Diana chuckled to herself. It was all happening just as a good fantasy should!

She leaned up on one elbow. Her robe fell open, and even in her dream, she could feel the coolness of the night breeze caress her breasts. She looked up at the shadowy figure above her and smiled.

"'How is it with you, milord?'" She asked, speaking a remembered line from Shakespeare.

"Well, milady. Well."

In the moonlight she could see his eyes roam over her body, lingering on the opening in her robe, the shadowy roundness of her breasts and the cleft in between. Diana shifted so that the robe gaped even more. Her eyes were adjusting to the moonlight, and she could see his pupils dilate and darken as his eyes devoured her. Seeing that desire made her bold.

"Captain Hawke, please, I must ask you something."

"Tomorrow, Lady Diana."

"No, now. It's urgent. Very important." She took his hand and drew him onto the bed beside her. In spite of his seeming reluctance, he came willingly. She could feel the warmth of his body next to hers. His white shirt gleamed eerily in the moonlight, and the black breeches clung to his strong thighs like a second skin.

Yet he still seemed cautious, as if he suspected a trick. Well, she did have a surprise in store for the staunch and stoic Captain Hawke, didn't she? Diana felt wonderfully warm, floating on a sea of sensuality.

She ran her hand along his thigh. Just touching him made her tingle with desire. Feeling the hard tautness of his muscles beneath the fabric of his breeches made her heart skip a beat as a delicious warmth flowed through her. And she felt wicked, very wicked indeed. She adored the feeling.

"Lean closer, Captain," she whispered. "I have something to ask you, but I must whisper."

He hesitated, his eyes clouded and wary. "Are you ill, or is this another one of your ruses?"

Diana only smiled, and that seemed to confuse him more.

"The door is locked," he said, "and this room is very far from the ground below. There is no escaping."

"Thank heavens for that." Why should she want to escape from this delicious dream?

She put her mouth close to his ear. His hair was soft against her face and smelled of soap and salt air. "I want to know...I must know...the answer to a question that has puzzled me for so long."

"And just what is that, milady?"

"I must know what you wear—beneath your breeches." As she spoke the words, she moved her fingers slowly up his thigh. "And this is probably my last chance to find out."

"My lady, you are ill with fever." He started to his feet, but Diana held on to his shirt with one hand and cupped his manhood with the other.

She heard his sharp intake of breath as she moved her fingers suggestively across the fabric of his breeches. "I would hazard a guess that you wear nothing at all, but how am I to know unless I see for myself?" She could feel him grow hard beneath her exploring hand, and the sensation of his arousal only added to the excitement that was coursing through her.

"God's breath, lady, you are a she devil. I should have known not to trust you."

His movement was quick, pinning her hands behind her head on the bed. Her bare breasts rubbed against the soft cotton of his shirt and the titillating feeling against her now-taut nipples sent little ripples of excitement through her.

"Cover yourself," he muttered.

"You're holding my hands," she reminded him.

He immediately released her. She clutched his shirt. "I don't intend to be covered up, Adam. I want to be completely uncovered, naked and hot in this big, soft bed. And I want you here, naked beside me."

The look on Captain Adam Hawke's face was one of torment, giving Diana a thrill of pleasure and of power. For the first time, she had the upper hand with her fantasy pirate.

When he spoke again, his voice was low and husky. "For the love of God, lady, you must understand that you are my hostage. Even though I am a renegade, I have always been a man of honor. I cannot—and I will not—ravage a woman in my protection."

"Damnation," Diana groaned. "It's my fantasy, and what do I end up with? A man of honor! Well, that's got to change and now."

She pulled him closer, feeling the hardness of his manhood against her thighs. His heart was beating as rapidly as hers, and his breathing was quick and rasping. No matter how honorable Captain Hawke's words, she could tell his actions were going to be just as lustful as hers.

"Kiss me, Adam, just once. Kiss me. Is that so difficult?"

She looked up at him, his handsome face framed by dark wavy hair. His eyes narrowed, and a sensual smile curved his lips. "Not difficult at all," he responded.

Then his mouth was hot on hers, moist, devouring. He released her hands and slipped his arms around her waist. Diana was flooded with heat and desire as she arched and molded her body more tightly to his. This was her fantasy, and she was going to enjoy every erotic moment of it.

5

DIANA PARTED her lips under his kiss. No dream had ever been more real, more erotic. She could feel his breath mingle with hers, and wanting to taste him thoroughly, she drew his tongue deep into her mouth. Adam responded eagerly and let his hands roam over her body as they kissed.

Diana moved her hands, too, tugging at the fabric of his shirt. "Too many clothes," she murmured against his mouth. He turned and shifted on the bed until he was no longer wrapped in her arms.

"No, Adam," she cried. "You can't leave me." She could hear the panic in her voice, but it didn't matter. She dared not release him—not in the middle of her dream—for fear he would disappear forever.

"Dear sweet Jesu, do you think that I could leave you now, when you torment me with your lips and drive me mad with your hands?" Tenderly he touched her cheek.

Diana remembered that soft touch from the first time his hand had grazed her cheek as they'd stood in the hallway at Fantasy Faire. That had been real, and this was a dream. Yet the touch was just the same; she melted beneath it.

"Adam . . ."

"Yes, milady?" The tips of his fingers brushed the taut tight bud of her exposed nipple.

Diana tried to speak, but no words would come. The dream became silent, as Adam took her nipple in his mouth. She touched his hair. It was soft and fine beneath her fingers, and the dual sensations of her hands in his hair and his lips on her breast caused Diana to catch her breath. There was a rising tide of excitement heating her blood and making her heart race.

He looked up at her, his eyes bright with desire. "Diana," he said huskily. "Diana . . ."

He hadn't spoken her name since her dream had begun, and the sound of it on his lips magnified the intensity of her feelings. Now he was moving his hand again, downward, sliding it along her abdomen to the damp heat at the joining of her thighs. He caressed her, exploring gently.

"You melt beneath me like honey, sweet and moist."

Diana had thought from their first kiss that she was truly melting, losing her bodily shape and flowing into Adam. Closer, she wanted to be closer. She tugged at his shirt. Looking up into his eyes, she saw the crinkly laugh lines that she remembered from reality. Now, here they were in her dream.

"Too many clothes," he mocked.

"Yes," she whispered, vainly pulling at his shirt, struggling to get closer to him.

Adam did it for her. She heard the cloth rip as he tore open his shirt. She heard the thump of his boots as they hit the floor. Through a haze, she saw him reach for the buttons of his breeches.

"No," she managed to say. Her voice was hoarse with desire. "I want to ..."

With trembling fingers, she worked at the buttons and slipped her hands into his trousers. His flesh was hot and damp. She took him in her hand, stroking him, feeling his erection grow beneath her eager touch.

With Adam's help, she pushed away his breeches. Moments later, the robe she wore slid from her body into a pool of silk on the floor, and she and her pirate lover were lying side by side, bodies touching, hands caressing, lips seeking and finding with greedy passion.

The pleasure was so intense that Diana thought she would die of it. His arousal was hard and strong against her. "Adam ..."

"Yes, Diana ..."

Their names, so intimate, so personal; their bodies, so naked and hot with need.

"I want you inside me. I want..." Her words trailed away on the edge of a moan as his fingers found that secret place within her and all thoughts were banished. There was only the sensation of his touch.

"Soon," he promised, "but first let me pleasure you in every way. I want to kiss you and taste you. . . ." He slid his tongue along her rib cage, licked the roundness of her abdomen, nibbled the line of her hipbone. His breath was hot upon her skin, and Diana held her breath, waiting, yearning. Then his mouth was on the moist place that hid the secret recesses of her passion.

She writhed beneath him, her head thrown back, little sounds of pleasure coming from somewhere deep inside as he explored her, deliberate and unhurried. It was torment, exquisite torment. His tongue caressed her with maddening slowness until her sighs of passion became cries of excitement, whimpers begging for release. He knew her needs. Magically he knew how to fulfill her.

He moved his mouth slowly, erotically, up the column of her body. His lips and tongue teased and tantalized. Her breasts felt swollen. Her nipples were tender and aching. Then his lips claimed hers, and in his kiss she tasted the very essence of her femininity.

She felt a desperate hunger for him, and she took him in her hand once more, greedily, longingly stroking his maleness.

"Oh, Diana," he whispered. "you torment me with your magic fingers."

Her voice was low and filled with passion. "No more than you torment me—"

He put his hand over hers. "Soon this shaft of mine will bring you more pleasure than my mouth and tongue."

"Now," she groaned. "Oh, now, Adam, before I die of need."

He slid inside her, and she opened to welcome him, drew him deep and enveloped him. He filled her completely, moving her to the edge of ecstasy, where the need was still infinitely great, powerful and all-consuming.

Adam moved slowly at first, looking down at her. She was lost in his dark, haunting eyes, and in the power of his body, the exquisite pleasure of his flesh against hers.

Diana arched her back to meet him, and his strokes became faster and deeper. She could hear the welcoming sounds made by her body as she took him inside, could even hear the pounding of their hearts and the mingling of their cries of need.

She wanted to be closer to him, to become a part of him, and she wrapped her legs around his back and her arms around his neck. She dug her fingers into his hot, moist flesh, held on to him and called his name as he plunged into her again and again. Diana's world was filled with Adam. Their rhythms matched; they were one.

Her release was powerful. Spiraling spasms of pleasure shook her, making her head swim and turning her body inside out. At the height of her passion, she felt Adam explode deep inside her, and she held on to him even more tightly while they rode out their exquisite pleasure.

They clung together on the rumpled sheets, slippery, passion damp, limbs entwined. His arms were around her waist; her leg was wedged between his. Two bodies in perfect harmony.

As she cuddled in the heat of his body, he pulled a cover over them. Diana lay quietly, listening to the sound of their harmonious breathing. Soon the dream would be over, but for now, it was quiet perfection, and she reveled in it.

"Only in my dreams . . ." she murmured, running her hand down the smooth muscles of his back.

"If this is a dream, I do not wish ever to wake up," he answered softly.

It was a dream, but how could he know that? He was only a figment of her imagination. Diana wanted to hold on to her fantasy, hold on to him. "Stay with me all night, Adam. Until I wake up. Stay with me. . . ."

Everything faded around her, and she never heard his answer.

"IT'S ONLY A DREAM—it's only a dream." Diana repeated the words as she ran frantically from the bed to the locked door to the barred window. "But if it's a dream, why can't I wake up?"

She'd expected to awaken at home in Orlando, curiously satisfied from her fantasy trip with Captain Adam Hawke. She was supposed to be in her room, with its brass bed and wicker furniture. Instead she was still on Rogue's Cay. Everything was the same as the night before. The little village lay before her, drowsing on the shore in the morning sun. The *Black Hawke* lay anchored on the turquoise blue sea. In the corner of the bedroom was the wooden tub where she'd bathed. Her robe lay discarded on the floor. And on the bed . . .

"Oh, no," she said aloud. On the bed was her fantasy pirate, Adam Hawke, totally nude.

Diana shut her eyes, pinched herself hard and opened her eyes again. He was still there, his long hard body sprawled proprietarily on the rumpled sheets. Her heart beat wildly, out of control, and her legs shook so hard that she could hardly stand.

This wasn't happening, she told herself. This couldn't be happening. Tentatively she crept across the floor toward Adam. If only he were just an apparition, left over from her dream. She touched him softly. Her nervous finger met what seemed to be real flesh, but he didn't move. Maybe there was still a chance this was her dream. She poked harder at his arm. He groaned and rolled over, and suddenly Diana began to scream.

He was out of bed in one quick movement. "My God, milady, what has happened to you?"

"You!" she shouted hysterically, "You're not supposed to be here. You're supposed to be a dream. Go away!"

She pushed at him, but when he didn't move, she began to beat hysterically on his chest with her closed fists.

"By thunder, that is enough!" He grabbed her shoulders and shook her hard. "You are acting like a madwoman." When she stopped screaming, he loosened his grip but didn't let go completely. "That is better, Diana," he said softly. "I do not want to have to restrain you."

"No," she said. "Of course not."

He lowered his hands, and as they stood staring at each other, the absurdity of the situation hit her. She was quite naked. So was Adam. But it wasn't their state of undress that concerned her as much as where they were.

"Help me," she cried out piteously to Adam. "Help me. I don't know what's going on. Please, tell me the truth."

He reached down, picked up the silk robe and held it for her to put on. Obediently Diana slipped into it and then moved away, walking a few steps before weakly leaning against the table, her head reeling. This couldn't be happening. But it was.

Through her haze of disbelief, she heard a knock at the door. She couldn't move, but Adam pulled on his trousers and strode across the room. He opened the door—and Diana screamed again.

It was the same wizened old woman. More proof that this wasn't a dream.

"Don't rightly know what to make of her, Cap'n," the old woman croaked as she stepped into the room.

"Nor do I, Mathilde."

"First she refused her vittles, now she makes the noise of all the hounds of Hell let loose."

Diana stopped her screaming. What good was it doing to scream? It wouldn't make them go away—Adam or the old woman.

Adam waved the woman farther into the room. "I do not know what has happened, Mathilde. Perhaps you can help the lady. I fear she has gone quite daft."

"She be needing a potion to calm her and return her to sleep."

Diana shook her head vehemently. "No! No potions. No wine. That's what started all my problems. I want coffee, and lots of it." Diana turned away from Adam and the old woman, but she retained her hold on the table. It was her security.

"As Lady Diana requests, Mathilde, bring her coffee."

"And you, Cap'n. What you be wantin'?"

"A pot of tea. Bring some food, too. I have a fearful hunger this morning."

He shot Diana a conspiratorial grin, but she ignored him as she finally let go of the table and sank into a nearby chair. She couldn't pretend any longer that she was living in a dream world. She wasn't. Either Adam Hawke was a psychotic charlatan of major proportions and truly believed he lived in the eighteenth century or...

The panic Diana had been pushing away slowly began to overtake her. She didn't want to face it; she knew it would send her into another fit of screams. Yet she had no choice.

"Mathilde," she called out to the old woman. "Can you tell me... what year is it?"

Mathilde paused and scratched her head with a scrawny finger. "I don't rightly know the year, lady, but I've been told that it's a new one just passed us by."

Adam sank into another chair opposite Diana. "Mathilde has little need to know the year. But I can tell you, milady."

"Yes?" Diana asked with trepidation.

"It is January of 1724."

Diana felt herself break out in a cold clammy sweat. For a moment she thought she might pass out, but she remained upright in her chair, her hands tensed. When she finally spoke, her voice sounded faint and far away.

"But...surely...I mean..." She struggled against the roaring in her head to form a complete sentence. "Mathilde, do you know the year when you were born?"

"Aye, that I do," the old woman announced proudly. "It be the year 1660 in London, the same one as our King George was born in."

The room started to spin. Diana wished she could believe that Mathilde was lying, but she knew in her heart that the old lady was truthful. She was too guileless, too unschooled for sophisticated game playing.

Diana leaned over, resting her face in her hands. "Coffee," she gasped. "And bring me a newspaper. I need to see the date."

"This is not London or Boston," Adam told her. "We have no newspaper. But we can provide you with sustenance." He turned to Mathilde and ordered her with a nod. "Be quick about it, old woman."

Then he reached across the low table and touched Diana's hair. She pulled away.

"Is my touch so odious?" he snapped. "Last night you seemed to delight in it. Or was last night, like today, some part of your feigned madness?"

Diana raised her head and stared at him. Last night. In the dawning horror of the day, she tried to push thoughts about it from her mind. Yet they persisted. Last night. In bed with Adam. She felt her face flame as she remembered the erotic words they'd spoken, the magic moments they'd shared, the incredible intimacies they'd enacted.

"Who are you?" she asked. "I mean, who are you really?"

"As I've told you since I brought you aboard the *Black Hawke*, I am Captain Adam Hawke, privateer and sometime renegade, wanted by the Crown—"

"And you really believe this is 1724?"

"Believe? Lady, I am not an unlettered servant like Mathilde. I know the year. I know George I sits upon the throne of England. I know the deputy governor of Maine is your godfather. I know—"

"There's something else you should know," Diana interrupted. "I'm not Lady Diana Tremont. I mean, I am Diana Tremont, but I'm far from royalty. Over the past two centuries, I'm sure there have been many people with the same name. Just as many people could be called Adam Hawke." She knew she was rambling, but she couldn't stop.

"Somehow a woman named Diana Tremont met a man named Adam Hawke. I was that woman—then. Except the man I met was a different Adam Hawke. We left Orlando and went to a gala aboard the replica of a sailing ship. There was lightning and a storm. I got hit on the head. Time got sort of mixed up, and now I'm here—"

"You make no sense at all, milady. Either you have a fever or perhaps the blow to your head caused a madness of a sort." A frown creased his forehead.

"No!" Diana shouted. "I'm not feverish, and I'm not mad. I'm Diana Tremont from Orlando, Florida. I live in the twentieth century, and somehow I got transported back in time."

"Talking that way, I do allow you must be mad."

"I don't want to believe this any more than you do, Adam. Time travel is for movies and TV. It's not really possible. I'm Diana Tremont. I'm a nineties woman. I own a shop called Fantasy Faire, and I don't believe in tarot cards or UFOs. And I certainly don't believe in time travel. So tell me, Adam," she said, looking him straight in the eye, "if there's no time travel, then how did I get here?"

"You got here, milady, on the *Black Hawke*—"

"Oh, for heaven's sake, you don't seem to understand what I'm saying. I've been transported back in time."

"This is not possible," he said lightly.

"Just what I've been saying. But possible or not, I'm here. And if I got here, I should be able to get back. All we need to do is figure out a way to reverse this time travel. It's got to be reversible, right? Because if it's not, I'm really going to go crazy. Raving, ranting bonkers."

"Bonkers?"

"Mad. Insane. Daft. That's a word you understand, isn't it? Oh, Adam, please, listen to me. I'm not Lady Diana. I'm another Diana from the future, and I—"

He smiled, crinkling the lines around his eyes, and Diana suddenly remembered the same laugh lines that she'd seen on the old Adam. The memory only caused her to be even more confused.

"Do you tell me that you're an apparition? A ghost of some kind? No, milady, the woman I shared a bed with was flesh and blood."

"I'm not a ghost. Of course not." Diana was infuriated that he couldn't seem to understand. "I'm real, but I'm from another time. Can't you get it through your head? I don't belong here, and I want to go back where I *do* belong."

"Enough, woman," he shouted, bringing his fist down hard on the table. "I will not let you go until the ransom is paid, no matter how many stories you tell me. Such is not possible. I know that. I am a rational man who knows much of the world. Your foolish fancies might be entertaining to those less educated, but not to me."

Footsteps sounded on the stairs. "And don't be talking of this to Mathilde. The mention of spirits frightens her."

"I don't want to talk about it to her—or to anyone. I want something to be done about it. I want *us* to do something about it."

She wondered why he couldn't grasp the horror of what was happening. By some terrible cosmic fluke, she'd been transported backward into another century, away from everything she knew and loved. It was mind shattering and so frightening that Diana wouldn't allow herself to explore all the ramifications of it for fear she would run—screaming again—from the room.

She couldn't do that because there was nowhere to run *to*. Her only choice was to deal with it as it happened. There was no way to anticipate, no way to prepare for what might come next or explain what had come before.

A respite was granted when the old lady entered, carrying a tray laden with fresh fruit, bread, pots of tea and coffee. With shaking hands, Diana poured herself coffee and drank it down hot and black.

Now was the time to try to explain to Adam, to make him understand what was happening to her— and get his help, somehow. There was no ignoring the fact that she was completely dependent upon him.

Adam poured his tea and covered a slab of bread with jam, all the while watching Diana through narrowed eyes. "You are a mystery, Lady Diana, a woman of many moods. You fight me, you make love to me and then you tell me tales—"

"Do not call me 'Lady Diana,'" she ordered through gritted teeth. "If I hear the word 'lady' one more time, I'll—"

"Commence screaming again?"

"Yes," she said. "Exactly. Because I'm just plain 'Diana.' That's what I want you to call me."

"'Tis agreed, although you are hardly plain."

He grinned, and she couldn't help noticing again, even in the midst of her terrible confusion, how damned attractive he was.

There was a long awkward silence. No matter how Diana tried to turn her head, the big canopied bed was still in her line of vision. This man had been her lover. It seemed impossible, but it had happened. She remembered everything, and his own words had verified it. Now she simply had to deal with it and forge some kind of relationship with this...this pirate who was holding her hostage in a way that he couldn't begin to fathom.

Diana's mind jumped frantically as she remembered parts of movies and television docudramas about people held hostage. She tried to remember the different ways they managed to escape. Obviously she couldn't overpower the man. Even though he'd put on his torn shirt again, the ripple of powerful muscles was evident.

Certainly madness, feigned or otherwise, wasn't going to impress Captain Adam Hawke. Maybe she should try to get him on her side, Diana thought. Wasn't that another one of the hostage's choices? Butter him up, act as if everything is normal, and wait for circumstances to change.

"So," she said in her best conversational tone, "were you born here in the Bahamas?"

Adam laughed at that. "No, milady, I am a relative newcomer to the island, but I have managed to make it my own. When my ship first landed here, Rogue's Cay was inhabited by a motley crew of wild-eyed shipwrecked buccaneers. They had set up a village of sorts. My men and I found that convenient. First we brought in our own booty and supplies. Then we moved people here, restless men, who did not necessarily see eye to eye with the laws of George I."

"And women?"

"Yes, women, too." Adam took a big bite from a mango, wiped his mouth with the back of his hand and held Diana's gaze as he spoke. "There is a longing for female companionship when a man has many months before the mast. You satisfied that longing for me last night."

Diana forced her eyes away.

"And, I find the need building again this morning. Look at me, Diana."

"No," she said firmly. She was determined to stick with her plan and make it work. There mustn't be any further mention of last night. "We were talking about you," she continued, "the women . . ."

"The longing. So." He bit into the fruit again. "They brought their women here. I take care of them all, men and women alike. They carry on business safely. I see to that."

"I bet you do." Diana found herself following his lead and reaching for a piece of fruit, a banana. She peeled it and for a moment savored the taste. It was sweet and meaty, not like the tasteless fruit she used to buy at the supermarket. "Where did you grow up if not here in the islands?"

"In the colonies."

"Oh," Diana said with surprise. That meant America.

"My father, Simon Hawke, was one of the finest shipbuilders in the colonies. He learned his trade in Liverpool at his own father's knee."

"Your family emigrated from England to the States?"

He frowned.

"I mean the colonies," Diana said, correcting herself.

Adam nodded. "In the village where I grew up everyone made a living from the sea—shipping, fishing, boat building. We were a prosperous village until the damned Navigation Laws took their toll."

"Navigation Laws? I remember something—" Diana thought back to her high-school history. She knew the British Navigation Laws had caused quite a stir in the colonies, but she was vague on the details.

Adam stood up, frowning at her quizzically. "Why should a highborn lady like yourself care about something that concerns only the working man?"

Diana opened her mouth and closed it immediately. This wasn't the time to comment on Adam's sexist remarks. Besides, she was determined to complete part one of her plan by getting on Adam's side. Then she'd worry about part two, whatever that might be.

"I know very little, but I'm curious," Diana said.

He turned toward her obligingly. "The laws, simply put, mean that goods from the colonies can be sold only in England—not at other ports on the continent. And we in the colonies can only buy goods from Britain, paying whatever customs tariff and duties the Crown decrees."

"Kind of like restriction on trade," Diana said. "So if someone in your village wanted to sell his...his..." She tried to think of what a villager might have to offer.

"His timber," Adam suggested, "to the people of Holland. The sale wouldn't be allowed. The timber must go to England—and at a lower price than could be obtained somewhere else."

"It sounds very unfair." Diana decided not to tell Adam the consequences of England's treatment of its colonial cousins, at least not yet.

"Unfair? It is bloody villainous," Adam spit contemptuously.

"So you became a pirate to get around the laws? I've heard about that—pirates who claimed to be on the side of righteousness."

He looked at her sternly. "Not a pirate. A privateer. And all perfectly legal, although I might not call it righteous, milady." He laughed. "I sailed under a Letter of Marque—"

"I know all about that," Diana interrupted.

"Of course, you do not."

"Of course, I do," Diana disagreed.

He stood, feet akimbo, hands on his waist, looking down and her and laughing with his eyes. "Then tell me, milady, just what is a Letter of Marque?"

Diana searched her brain and came up with the answer, straight from a social-studies textbook. "An agreement with a high government official—"

"How do you know that?" He seemed furious.

"I learned it in school," she told him.

"You—a woman?"

"Yes, me—a woman," she cried. "Do you think I'm a complete dope?"

"Dope?" he repeated.

"Idiot, lunatic, whatever you call it in your century!"

He waited, staring down at her.

"Okay, the letter was, well, permission, of a sort to take prize ships, enemies of England that were usually French or Spanish, confiscate all the stuff they were carrying and take it back to sell in the States— uh, colonies."

"What do you mean by all the—stuff?" he asked.

"Booty, I guess you call it."

"Indeed we do." He grinned again. "Our booty came from a captured Spanish galleon that we sailed back to my village in Maine. Since the goods were Spanish, we saw no reason to notify customs or the tax collector of our return. We were acting as free men."

"Rebelling against the British," Diana observed. "I'm not surprised. It's the way our country was founded."

"Our country?"

"The colonies, I mean."

"In the colonies only the rich—or the rebellious— have a chance to win." There was real bitterness in his voice.

"And you weren't rich?"

Adam threw back his head and laughed. "No, milady, and that leaves only—"

"Rebellious." She joined in the laughter, which stopped abruptly. "But something happened—"

"Yes." His eyes had a hard glint. "This is the part you should know right well, Lady Diana, despite your protestations. Naval officers were waiting for us. The official who had signed my Letter of Marque denied it. He declared the letter a forgery and I and my men not privateers but pirates."

"You could have been hanged!"

"Indeed I would have gone to the gallows had not the good people of the village helped me escape. Come here," he said, holding out his hand.

Diana, who'd had no intention of responding to that order, found herself moving toward Adam. He stood by the window.

"What do you see there?"

She looked out. "The harbor. The village that you dragged me through." She gave him a sideways glance, to which he didn't respond. "A ship at anchor."

"All mine."

"Then why should you be concerned about what happened in a little Maine seaport? You have everything here."

"No, milady. Do let me finish my story."

Diana was agreeable. It was a kind of bizarre history in the making, but in reverse.

"The Spanish booty was impounded," he told her, "and my father's shipyard confiscated. He was imprisoned. Unlike myself, he has not escaped. Now do you see that what I have here counts for nothing when my own father is in chains?"

"Isn't there anything you can do—an appeal to the Crown?"

Adam shook his head.

"Then surely some high-up official can help you."

He laughed then, a cold hard laugh. "Your jest falls short, milady, for you know full well that the man who is the most high up, the man who has infinite power . . ."

"Yes?"

"Is your godfather. . . ."

"Adam, how many times do I have to tell you? I don't have a godfather."

"Then answer me this. How do you know so much about the Letters of Marque?"

"I know because I read about them in school."

"By the powers, I do not believe that!"

"Well, believe it or not, it's true. For some reason— I don't have any idea why—I remembered."

"Balderdash," he said.

"Maybe I remembered because of my fantasy—"

"You're talking craziness again," he told her.

"That's it. This whole pirate fantasy made me remember everything about the high seas in the eighteenth century," she said, for herself more than for Adam.

"Then remember this," he ordered. "Sir Winston Grenville, deputy governor of Maine, ruined my father, drove my mother from her home, turned me into an outlaw and even now holds my father in chains. That same Sir Winston Grenville is your godfather, deny it as you will. He holds my father captive! Do you understand that much?"

Diana understood and a terrible sense of foreboding overwhelmed her. "It's not money you're holding me for, is it? You want to trade me for your father."

Adam's black eyes glittered dangerously. "I would do anything to set my father free."

Diana felt her body sag. He reached out to steady her, but she turned away from him and walked back across the room, whispering to herself, "That's why I'm here. That's why I'm here! I'm Simon Hawke's ticket to freedom."

6

"YOU LOOK PALE, lady, as if you might swoon." Adam seemed more irritated than concerned.

"I need air, please." Diana felt claustrophobic. "I've been in this room so long I can't breathe. Please, Adam," she begged.

With a shrug, he agreed, then led her down the stairs, through a hall and into a small garden adjoining the courtyard. Diana sat on a marble bench nestled among the tropical flowers.

"So you see why I must keep you safe and secure until the exchange is complete," Adam said. "Even now, the ransom letter is on its way to your godfather."

Diana looked at him with dawning horror in her eyes. His story wasn't fabricated; she could tell that. He'd told it with total honesty. She was a hostage on an island in the middle of nowhere. Adam Hawke was the only man who could free her. If and when he chose to do so, he'd turn her over to her godfather, a man she was beginning to fear more and more.

And no matter what happened, she was still in the eighteenth century!

She wet her lips nervously with the tip of her tongue. "So tell me, Adam, how long will this exchange take?"

"That is difficult to say."

"Weeks?" she asked. "Months?"

"Not so long, I believe. After all, Grenville will be eager to retrieve his godchild, the daughter of his closest friend."

"Oh, sure. Good old Godfather Winston."

Adam sat down beside her and stretched out his legs. "There is one problem, however. I am no longer eager to make this trade. I see you differently now, especially after last night." He turned his dark eyes in Diana's direction. "I had no idea you would be such a willing captive."

"I'm not—"

He wasn't listening. "It would be pleasurable for us both if we extended your stay on Rogue's Cay."

Diana's nervousness intensified. Adam reached out and grazed her cheek with that old familiar touch she remembered from another century.

"Adam—"

Silently he traced the line of her collarbone. His hand was dangerously near her breast. Diana tried to move away, but it was too late. She was already under his spell. A fluttering inside her was followed by a burst of heat and longing.

Adam's voice was seductive. "Yes, Diana?"

"This isn't right...."

"There are no rules on Rogue's Cay about making love, Diana. The daylight has its own special delights—"

Diana closed her eyes as Adam slid his hand lower, brushing her nipple. She felt it harden under his touch, and she shivered with excitement. Her body felt like it was on fire as she felt herself sink into a languorous softness. . . .

"No!" she said suddenly, moving away from him.

Adam's eyes flickered with surprise, and there was a hard edge to his voice. "You had no objections last night, milady. In fact, you drew me to your bed. You made me forget that you were my hostage and that lovemaking between us should not occur. You made me forget everything." His voice softened. "I am very glad that I forgot."

"That was last night," she explained, "and you weren't real then. I mean, you were there, but I didn't know who you were. Now that I know you're real, I should realize that our lovemaking was also real, not a fantasy, but I don't want to. Oh, hell, I'm not explaining this very well, am I?"

"Frankly, you are talking like a madwoman." He stood up and moved away from the bench.

Diana found herself standing, too. She approached him, trying to organize her thoughts. "Please understand, Adam, I don't know you at all—"

He laughed softly. "I believe that we know each other well, milady, very well. We learned much last night—" He looked at her through narrowed eyes. "You were as lusty as any serving wench. It was a real surprise to find such a woman. On the outside a regal lady, in bed a—"

Diana groaned. "Oh, please, Adam. I don't want to talk about last night."

He persisted. "I did not realize that the highborn Lady Diana would be a woman of . . . some experience. I thought your kind was kept safe and guarded for the wedding night."

"Lady Diana Tremont might well be a virgin. For all I know, *she* might wear a chastity belt. But since I'm not Lady Diana—" She broke off and spoke almost defiantly. "Yes, I've been in love. I've had a lover. But that was years ago, and it's none of your business."

"You are right, milady. I should not judge, certainly not one so young."

"Young? I'm twenty-six, old enough to have lived a little." She flung her hands up in frustration. "Why am I bothering to explain this to you?"

"Twenty and six?" His surprise was evident. "Why, by your teeth and the softness of your skin, I thought you no more than one and twenty."

"Thanks to modern dentistry and cosmetics," Diana muttered. "You see, Adam, all this goes to show the wide gap between us. You don't understand about the twentieth century, and I don't want to know any more about the eighteenth! Now that I understand the reality of the situation—or what I think is the reality—anything between us is impossible. Don't you see? I was pretending—"

He grabbed her arm and swung her around. "You are lying, milady."

The sun hit her in the face with blinding intensity. She lifted her arm to protect her eyes, and he caught her wrist.

"What happened between us was no pretense. It was real and lustful and filled with passion. And you know it."

Diana's eyes burned less from the sun than from her embarrassment. "Yes, it was all those things," she admitted, "but it was also wrong. I didn't understand that this was really happening—"

Diana looked around at the little courtyard that was clearly from another time. "I just didn't understand," she repeated softly before turning back to him. "You're a man of honor, and because I'm your hostage and you must protect me, I ask that you respect my privacy." She dropped her eyes to avoid his gaze. "My bedroom must be mine and mine alone. I won't share my bed with you."

Diana tried to pull away from him, but he held on as if to prove that his superior strength made him master of both her and the situation.

When he responded, his eyes were contemptuous. "I shall respect your wishes, milady." He released her arms and gave a familiar mocking, bow. "But let me remind you, this house and everything within it is mine." He paused as if to let that sink in. "I will escort you back to your room now," he said coolly, taking her arm.

When he left her at the door, Diana stepped into the room and paused, listening for the inevitable sound that came immediately—the clink of the key turning in the lock. In a surge of emotion, she threw herself across the bed and burst into tears.

THE NEXT MORNING, to her amazement, Diana found her door unlocked. She hurriedly dressed and stepped outside her room, relishing the freedom. As she wandered along the hall Mathilde called out.

"Lady, lady! The cap'n left no word for you to go roamin' around the house."

"He unlocked the door for me," Diana said, "and yet all I can do is roam around the house." There was a dark sadness in her voice. "I can't get off this island." She smiled ruefully to herself. "Unless of course an airline terminal has been built overnight."

Throwing up her arms in exasperation, Mathilde turned on her heel and started down the hall in the direction she'd come from. Diana was hot on her heels.

"Are you going to the kitchen?" Diana asked as she caught up with the scrawny woman.

"I reckon," came the reply.

"I'll go with you."

"Do as you please. I've no time to pay heed to ye."

"Then you won't object if I make myself some breakfast," Diana said.

"It's long gone past breakfast time."

"Then lunch. Maybe a salad—made from the greens in the fridge?" A perverse stubborn streak made her joke. There was little else to do after lying across her bed and crying until she had no tears left. Obviously crying wasn't the answer, and keeping her sense of humor seemed one way to hold on to sanity.

"Cap'n said you'd be talking daft and to pay no heed. Reckon I can warm you up a piece of roast beef from last night—"

"Nope, I'm trying to cut down on red meat. Doctor's orders. Cholesterol, you know." *Stop it, Diana,* she ordered herself. *You aren't amusing anyone.*

Diana followed Mathilde through a narrow side yard, across another courtyard and into a big damp kitchen.

Mathilde turned her attention to the wooden slab, where she began attacking a large fish.

"What about that?" Diana asked. "Let's fillet the fish, and I'll show you how to cook it Cajun style. You know, blackened with lots of pepper." Diana looked around the kitchen. "I'm sure you have pepper."

Mathilde's mouth tightened. "Cap'n said nothing 'bout you helpin' in the kitchen. I cook the meals here, and this fish goes in the cap'n's stew.

"I guess he's the boss, then." Diana sneaked a banana from a wooden bowl.

"Aye, that he be, and he won't sanction the likes of ye in me kitchen. Nor will he like them clothes ye be wearin',"

"You found them for me, so take responsibility."
Diana shrugged and peeled the banana. The Fantasy
Faire gown was a total loss, so she'd finally cajoled
Mathilde into rummaging through the servants'
quarters and coming up with an outfit for her. She'd
managed to fit into the white blouse and loosely wo-
ven brown skirt, even though the blouse was a trifle
small and the skirt too short. It was close enough to
the twentieth century to suit her fine, and at least the
outfit was comfortable.

"Where is he, anyway?" Diana hadn't seen Adam
since their last scene together in the courtyard. He'd
taken her at her word and left her alone, sending
Mathilde and a young serving girl to minister to her
needs.

"I reckon he's takin' care of things like other folks
ought to be doin'."

"I get the message," Diana muttered. "Sure you
don't want to try Cajun-style fish?" At Mathilde's
fierce look, Diana left the kitchen and wandered into
the courtyard. Climbing a stone staircase, she found
herself on a balcony near the back of the house. The
Caribbean glistened in the sun beyond a half-moon
curve of pure white beach secluded below the house
at the bottom of a steep cliff. Palmetto, palm and banana trees swayed in the breeze, and on the air she
caught the scent of orange blossoms.

"Club Med, eat your heart out," Diana murmured, crossing to the broad railing and hoisting herself up. Tourists would pay thousands to travel to a

place like this, she thought. And just about now, Diana would pay millions to get away.

She was thankful, however, that Adam had unlocked her door this morning. She'd been on the verge of going stir-crazy with nothing to read, no paper for writing or sketching and no one to talk to except Mathilde, who was hardly a scintillating conversationalist.

The day before she'd told Adam to leave her alone, and he had. Wasn't that exactly what she wanted? He was too dangerous and unsettling and...just too sexy to be around. At the same time, she was irritated that he didn't make more of an effort to see her. She was dependent upon him as she'd never been dependent on anyone.

"He could at least have the decency to stop by and see if I need anything," Diana said aloud, and then burst into laughter. She was talking to herself again; it was getting to be a habit—just one more sign that she was probably going off her rocker.

Diana knew she couldn't sit still long. She was too anxious and unsettled. And worried. Not only about herself but about her parents, about Mindy, Harry, Fantasy Faire and Adam—the other Adam.

Agitated, Diana slid off the railing and began to prowl up and down the balcony. She stopped before double oak doors leading to a room she knew immediately to be Adam's. One of the doors seemed to be ajar. She stepped closer. It was definitely cracked.

Boldly, she pushed it inward. The light streamed into the room, following the trajectory of the door.

She peered inside. A huge carved mahogany bed dominated the room, its canopy draped with mosquito netting. She slipped inside, walked past the bed to a table strewn with charts and maps and the strange kind of nautical equipment she'd noticed on the *Black Hawke*. She bent over the maps, hoping to find something recognizable, something from the world she knew. There was nothing except ancient squiggles and numbers. She couldn't even pick out Rogue's Cay or figure how far away she was from help.

She moved on, too quickly, and collided with the sharp brass edge of a large trunk at the foot of Adam's bed. Rubbing her knee, she sat on a stool and found herself opposite a low bookcase. Surprised to see it crammed with beautifully bound volumes of soft leather, Diana felt in her element. She chose a book from the shelf and opened it. *The Life and Strange Surprising Adventures of Robinson Crusoe, of York, Mariner....* She noted the date, 1719.

"Which of my books intrigues you, milady?"

Startled at the voice behind her, Diana dropped the book and jumped guiltily to her feet. He'd come into the room as stealthily as a cat. Diana tried to stay calm, reminding herself not to be caught off guard again. "*Robinson Crusoe*. I did a book report on it in tenth grade, but I'm afraid I never quite finished it," she answered.

"Book report?"

"Never mind." Diana leaned down and picked up the book. "Do you know this is a first edition?" She held it out to him. "It's worth a lot of money."

"I do not know why the monetary value of my book should concern you, milady, but in any case, I have no plans to sell it. My library is for my reading pleasure."

Diana clutched the book to her. "May I borrow it?"

"Of course." He stood for a moment, evaluating her with his penetrating gaze. "Why are you dressed like a scullery wench? I told Mathilde to clean and repair your clothing."

"It was beyond repair. I thought these clothes would be more suitable for…ah, just kind of hanging around the house."

He perused her again, this time more slowly, starting at her bare feet and ankles. His eyes traveled up the length of her body and then stopped, fixated on her breasts. Diana could feel the heat of his gaze washing over her.

Suddenly vulnerable, she hunched her shoulders forward. Was it her fault she didn't have a bra? The thin fabric of her blouse stretched tightly across her breasts. She glanced down and felt really humiliated. The roundness of her breasts was outlined by the tightly stretched fabric and her nipples seemed to stand straight up.

Diana's face flushed as she raised her eyes and met Adam's wolfish, mocking look.

"I would suggest you avail yourself of a shawl," he said dryly, "before you venture out in public."

"I can go out alone?"

"Of course. Is your door not unlocked?"

"Yes, but I didn't realize I could leave the house."

"You may go wherever you wish. There is no way for you to leave the island without assistance, and no one here will be willing to help you."

Diana didn't care. Just the news that she could go out on her own made her feel free. "Thank you, Adam."

"'Tis nothing. And now, if you have finished searching my room . . ."

"I wasn't searching," she argued. "I was just curious—"

He leaned back against the table. "The last time I spoke with you, I was ordered out of your sight." He folded his arms across his chest and raised a dark eyebrow quizzically. "Now I find you ransacking my bedroom."

"How could I know it was your bedroom?" she asked. "There's no sign."

Adam laughed. "No, milady, there is not a sign, but somehow I suspect you knew."

"That's very arrogant of you."

He laughed but didn't disagree. "Still," he said, reaching out to run his curved fingers down the side of her face. "I think you were interested in the room where I sleep."

"No, I—"

"Yes, Diana."

She couldn't retreat. Her back was against the wall, and Adam had her cornered. Her skin tingled where he'd touched her, and she wondered again what it was about this man that threw her so off base. Was it his brazenness, his brashness, his authority? She hated the power Adam had over her, the power that was so evident even in something as casual as a touch.

She pushed his hand away and glared at him, fighting for some authority of her own, but his eyes just gleamed with laughter. Even worse, his body fairly vibrated with vitality. He wore a vest over his white shirt and a bright-red scarf knotted at his neck. She knew what was below the clothes—the body that had been hot and muscular against her. The memory flooded over her. She fought against the quivering that began in the pit of her stomach and started to spread, slowly, agonizingly.

"I was bored," she said stubbornly. "And now that I have something to read—"

"Were books all you searched for," he persisted, "something to read? I did not know my captive was a scholar."

Diana bristled. "The problem is that you're even holding a captive." The forcefulness of her words was meant to deflect the feeling of sexual awareness that smoldered between them. "That's the coward's way!" she flung the words at him.

His jaw tightened, and the warmth in his eyes drained away. "It is the only way left to me. And I need no lessons in courage from the goddaughter of Winston Grenville."

Diana held her own. "Captive or not, I won't be daunted by you, and you would be wise to listen to what I have to say. You might just learn something, Captain Hawke."

Diana thought she saw a flicker of admiration in his eyes. Then his expression shifted and hardened.

"Oh, I have learned from you, milady. I have learned that under cover of darkness Lady Diana is a woman of infinite passions, but in daylight she chooses to play the role of crazed peasant girl talking of spirits from another world—"

"Another century, Adam, not another world!" Diana tried to push past him, but he blocked her with his body. "Get out of my way, Adam Hawke. You don't have a clue about what's going on, not a clue."

"Yet truly I know what goes on between men and women, milady. It is you who pretends not to know."

They glared at each other, and Diana suddenly realized that he could scoop her up, as he'd done before, and carry her to his bed. "Oh, I know all right. Let me give you my answer in a language that you understand, or pretend to. Step aside! Avast, you . . . you knave!"

She shoved him with all her might and, still clutching the book, ran from his bedroom, down the hall and up the stairway to her room.

Inside, Diana leaned back against the door. "Damn," she cried, "he's got me talking like someone from a bad pirate movie. Bastard," she added under her breath. "And worse, now I'm cursing like a sailor, too! Somehow I've got to get out of here."

WHEN SHE WAS sure that Adam had left the house, Diana searched out Mathilde and did some judicious bargaining. The old woman didn't argue, so Diana knew Adam had given instructions that the prisoner be allowed whatever she wanted. That's how she managed to start her trek to the village outfitted with a colorful shawl, a basket for her purchases and a kerchief with a coin of every denomination knotted inside. Just another villager, off to the market, Diana told herself. But for this villager, there was method in what Adam would certainly call her madness.

And the madness persisted, if it was madness, leading Diana to imagine that Rogue's Cay was not just an island in the Caribbean but an island in time. If she could escape, she would find herself back in the twentieth century. In her topsy-turvy Alice in Wonderland world, anything was possible.

She'd barely set foot in the little village, when the cadence began.

"Melons as sweet as a woman's breasts," a shopkeeper called out, "and for the captain's special lady, a special gift."

"Come into my shop, your ladyship, and see the pretty dresses, suitable for the captain's favored one."

"For the captain's lady..."

"The captain's lady..."

Diana found herself being jostled from store to store amid the laughter and cheering. Clearly everyone in the village recognized her immediately, and furthermore, they seemed to know what had passed between her and Adam. She shouldn't have been surprised. Mathilde . . . the other servants . . . Gossip didn't change through the centuries.

Diana walked among them, her smile in place, until a tall woman moved from the crowd and stopped in front of her. Diana thought she could hear the intake of breaths all around her.

The woman wore a brightly patterned dress and had curling black hair cascading down her back. Her brown eyes glittered with hostility as she moved back and forth in front of Diana, one of her hands concealing something in the folds of her skirt.

Diana took a step backward, knowing instinctively that this woman was her enemy.

A murmur went through the crowd, and Diana heard the name repeated again and again, *La Perla*. *La Perla*. The woman tossed her head before speaking. Her voice was a deep contralto. "Ye are not as pretty as I imagined. 'Tis a puzzle that he chooses your bed o'er mine."

Diana's heart thumped loudly. There was no point in denying that charge; obviously everyone knew it. She stood tall. "Now, listen to me La Pearl, or whatever you're called. I don't want your captain. You can have him in your bed any night. Take him, he's yours!"

"Liar!" La Perla began to circle Diana with a cat-like grace. "I can in no wise believe your words. Ye want him, ye and every woman on this island."

In one lightning movement, she drew her hand from the folds of her skirt, and the blade of a knife glittered in the sun.

The basket dropped from Diana's hands, and she tried to move back, but the crowed pushed against her. "There's been a terrible mistake," she cried. "I shouldn't even be here. I'm from another century, and if you help me leave, you can have him for your-self—"

Diana let out a breath that turned into a half scream as La Perla feinted toward her with the knife, pulled back and then came on again. The knife slashed through the air, cutting a silvery path only inches from Diana's outstretched arm.

Instinctively she sidestepped, keeping her arms raised in a defensive position. "All right, La Perla, you're in for it now. I've studied karate! I'm almost a black belt."

That last part wasn't true, but Diana and Mindy *had* taken a six-week course in self defense when they'd decided to keep Fantasy Faire open at night.

"Aha!" Diana moved sideways with an appropriate noise. Even as she wove and bobbed, remembering that a moving target was hard to hit, Diana's mind was screaming. The dream had turned into a nightmare—and she couldn't wake up!

La Perla seemed confused at the whirling, darting form before her. Diana was encouraged. She tried to recall her classes. Why hadn't she paid more attention? Her hands were useless as weapons, but the short skirt freed her legs.... That reminded her—there was a way to topple her opponent!

The pressure point was behind and a little above the knee. A hard kick there could send La Perla to her knees. In class, Diana had always been afraid to use her full strength, and now she wasn't even sure where the pressure point was.

The other woman swore and crouched low, imitating Diana. The knife blade seemed much larger from this angle, and seeing the glint, Diana forgot all about self-defense and did the sensible thing. She screamed.

"Help me—someone help! Grab her—take away the knife and hold her down!"

Instead of coming to her rescue, Diana realized people were making bets! Nothing short of a miracle could help her now.

The dark-haired woman made a thrust forward, and Diana responded like a star pupil at last, swinging her leg out and going for the pressure point. There was a thud as she made contact.

With a stunned look, La Perla groaned and crumpled to the ground. Diana rushed forward and kicked the knife away. She'd seen that in a hundred movies but couldn't believe she was actually doing it herself.

The knife spiraled through the air and landed at the edge of the crowd. La Perla sprawled on her back, and with a shriek of triumph, Diana fell on her. She'd never been in a fight and had no idea where the primitive impulse came from, but she straddled La Perla and grabbed her hair. La Perla screamed invectives and tried to free herself; Diana held, and the crowd roared its approval.

The moment of glory was short-lived as a strong arm looped around Diana's waist and pulled her to her feet.

"God's breath, what are you wenches doing?"

There was no doubt Adam Hawke was furious. He kept a firm hold on a struggling Diana as he shouted to his companion, "Russell, get that hellcat off the ground and out of here."

A dazed La Perla was struggling to her feet. "Cap'n," she cried, "I was thinking of ye, only ye. We belong together—"

"Take her away, Russell. Now!"

As Russell Karlan and another man dragged a hysterical La Perla away, Adam's voice rang out. "Lady Diana is our hostage. I want no harm to come to her while she is under my care. I will deal harshly with anyone, man or woman, who touches her. Let that suffice!"

7

AS IF BY MAGIC, the crowd melted away under Adam's wrath, fading into shops and houses, disappearing down alleyways and along the beach.

That's when Adam turned on Diana. "And you, fighting like a common street urchin. My God, lady, what came over you?"

Without waiting for an answer, he began to drag Diana along the street. "I will lock you in your room and this time throw away the key. You cannot be trusted."

Halfway down the street Diana managed to dig her heels into the dirt and slow him down. "Don't you realize what I've been through? I've just been in a knife fight! Do you think I do that every day?"

Without responding, he grabbed her again, but she shrugged him off. "I won't be dragged up that hill another time. I'll walk beside you on my own."

Without a word and with anger still brewing, Adam released her arm and started up the hill at a fast clip.

"Your . . . your girlfriend was trying to kill me," Diana called after him. "You know that, don't you?"

When she got no response, she went on, "I've been attacked by a madwoman, and here you are treating me like I was the one at fault...."

Adam had quickened his steps, and Diana struggled to keep up with him.

"Like I'm a damned criminal," she yelled after him. "Well, isn't that the way? Blame the victim—take out your hostilities on me, when you should—"

They'd reached the shadow of the house. Adam kicked open the door, but before he had a chance to shove her inside, Diana walked past him, head high, and then turned back, looking over her shoulder at him. "And do you know what else?" she cried out as he followed her into the house. "I could have won! I had her down, without a knife—I could have won!"

Diana leaned against the cool wall of the entranceway, her breath coming in short bursts. She was excited and more alive than she'd ever been. She'd survived a fight, defended herself and nearly been victorious!

"And do you know what?" he mocked her. "You could also have been killed."

Breathing hard himself, Adam leaned against the wall next to Diana. Then he turned her around and placed one hand against the wall near her shoulder, caging her with his body. "Your hotheaded behavior angers me mightily," he said. Yet it wasn't anger she saw in his eyes.

"Do you realize how foolish you were to indulge in such behavior with a woman like La Perla?" he continued.

She could feel the heat of his body; his physical presence was overwhelming. "You're the one who's been 'indulging' her." Adrenaline raced through Diana. If Adam seemed menacing to her, she felt reckless and wild beside him.

"Hardly, milady," he responded, leaning forward so that his knee found a resting place between her legs. "You are my charge. It is you I must watch over."

"I can take care of myself. I've proved that!"

Adam smiled down at her, condescendingly, she thought.

"I can get off this damn island, too, someway, somehow...."

But at this moment, she couldn't even dislodge herself from the nearness of his body.

"I fought La Perla, and I won—"

"The battle was not over," he reminded her.

"I almost won. I could have won if you hadn't stopped me. And I can fight you—"

"You are fighting me now."

"And I won't let you win, I won't let you dominate me." Her heart was racing, her temperature rising with each empty threat.

"This does not concern battles, Diana. This is about us, the fire that leaps between us like lightning—"

"Lightning..." She remembered the lightning that had accompanied their first kiss in that other world, that other time.

"Yes, lightning. It crashes around us when I hold you—"

"It was there that night, Adam."

"Yes," he said.

His mouth came down on hers, hot and demanding. His tongue invaded her lips, and his taste mingled with hers. Diana gave a little moan as she tried to recapture that other time, but it was gone quickly, blotted out by Adam, here and now. There was nothing to compare with what she felt at this moment, with this man. The passion caught fire. It was inescapable.

She wrapped her arms tightly around his neck. He lifted her, and her legs locked around his hips. They were completely entangled, completely ablaze.

Diana felt a thousand sensations at once—the insistence of his erection hard against her, the long slow quiver of desire flowing through her blood, his lips against her neck, then damply on the fabric of her blouse, the heat, consuming, deep inside. All those sensations flowed together and then blossomed until she was consumed by need for him.

"We...won't...we...can't make it to the bedroom...." Her words were strangled.

"No, milady, there will be no bed for us this day."

He lowered her to the floor, and Diana held up her arms to draw him close.

Diana could feel the cold, hard tiles of the marble floor beneath her, but only for a moment. Then the moment was gone and she forgot they were in the hallway of Adam's house. It had become their sanctuary where their only thoughts were physical and lustful, filled with need and desire.

Struggling together, they pushed her clothes aside—skirt pushed up to her waist, panties pulled to her ankles, blouse opened to reveal her breasts. Then Adam helped Diana unbutton his breeches and release his erection into her waiting hands. Its heat flared through her; from the fingertips upward, her blood turned to hot wine.

There was no hesitation, no moment of indecision. They became one in an instant as the driving need plunged them together. Hot and moist, hands grasped skin, mouths licked and sucked, legs and arms were entwined. He plunged into her with all his force, and she was ready for him.

There was nothing dreamlike about this. It was very real, and it was what she wanted, all she wanted. At first he'd been her fantasy: now he was flesh and blood, heat and fire. There was no controlling their lovemaking; it was primeval and primitive, as inevitable as the rising sun.

They moved together, bodies locked, their moans of passion filling the room. The pleasure was more than Diana had ever known, so intense that she knew it must end even as she wanted it to last forever. Then she felt it—the explosive tempo rushing to the core of her being. There was no controlling the shattering pleasure that ripped through her and left her breathless in his arms.

She could still feel his manhood inside her, and she didn't want to lose him. "Kiss me, Adam," she whispered. "Kiss me now, and please don't ever stop."

His mouth was on hers, his arms cradling her, as he carried her down the hall and kicked open the door to his room. He placed her gently on the bed and then lay down beside her. He was big and strong and warm, and she clung desperately to him.

"Diana, you are trembling."

"Yes."

"Are you all right? Did I hurt you?"

"Oh, no, Adam, no."

He stroked her hair, which was still damp from their lovemaking. "Ah, sweet Diana. I have never felt such pleasure."

"Neither have I," she murmured. "You give me so much joy."

"And yet you still tremble."

She snuggled closer. "I'm scared, Adam."

"Not of me?" He held her tightly and kissed her tenderly.

"No, never of you. I'm frightened of what's happening between us. I want you so much that it scares me to death."

"To death?"

Diana laughed softly. "That's only an expression. Still," she mused, "I am frightened."

"That's a mad notion you have, Diana."

He gathered her up into his arms and pulled her across his lap, peeling off the rest of her clothes until she was naked and warm in his arms. With one hand he smoothed back her hair again. Then he chuckled; she could hear the sound rumbling in his chest.

"What is so funny?"

"It is not really amusing. And yet I laugh, possibly because I need to make light of what I am feeling."

"Which is . . ."

"I believe that I am . . . a little frightened, too."

She lifted her face to his and kissed him long and hard. "I can't believe that anything would ever frighten you—"

"Nothing real, not musket or sword. But something unfathomable. . . ."

She looked into his eyes.

"The untamable, always fascinating spirit of Lady Diana Tremont. Who may even *be* a spirit, and who never does what I expect."

"Spirit or not," she said, nibbling on his ear, "I don't believe you're frightened of me."

"But you cannot be sure. . . ."

"No," she admitted.

"Because you do not really know me." There was a glimmer of laughter in his eyes as his hand drifted from her hair, along her shoulder. "Are you a spirit, Diana?"

"I'm not sure—of anything. That's what frightens *me*."

"Nor am I. Perhaps we should not think about it now." He moved his hand downward to her breast and caressed her gently.

Diana felt as though she were dissolving against him. "What do you suggest we do, instead?" She let her hand wander down his body.

"Why, Lady Diana, could you be teasing me?"

"Yes, Captain, I could just be," she replied brazenly.

Adam dampened her breast with his lips, kissing a trail to her nipple. His breath was warm and moist against her skin. They were immersed in both mystery and magic, but as she opened herself to Adam's lovemaking, she thought only of the magic.

"IT'S DARK OUTSIDE," Diana noted, propping herself up on her elbow. "How did that happen?"

"Magically," he said.

"No, let's not talk about magic—"

"Or spirits?"

"Or spirits . . . or anything otherworldly. Let's just talk of reality, of now and of us, you and me."

"Then I will answer you easily, my dear Diana. Night comes when two people spend most of the day in bed."

"Shamelessly in bed," Diana said, correcting him. Her lips curved in a smile. She and Adam had been shameless in their exploration of each other. She caressed his chest, luxuriating in the silky hairs across his taut skin and the lean muscles beneath. She loved to touch him; his body seemed to pull her hands like a magnet.

She'd often heard about men and women drawn together in love affairs that seemed predestined, but she'd dismissed the idea as absurd. Obsession was a weakness, Diana had always believed. At least until now. Until Adam.

Yet there was more than her physical need of him. She desired him in many other ways. He was her fantasy lover, the man who satisfied her as no one ever had. At the same time, he was her lifeline, the only reality she had to hang on to in the new world into which she'd been hurled.

Adam admitted his own bewilderment. "Truly, I am confused at this strange turn of events. In the beginning, you were only my hostage. But now you are much more, and the circumstances have become so complex."

Diana squirmed, feeling anxious and uncomfortable. As long as they were making love, she could forget that her so-called godfather was his mortal enemy. "And yet, I'm still your hostage," she said, pushing back the covers and searching for her clothes in the gathering darkness. "Oh, Adam, this is so strange." She pulled on her blouse. "I don't think you have any idea how strange it is."

"I believe I do."

"I'm not a normal hostage. Am I?"

Adam smiled. "I am not sure. You are my first hostage."

"Then let's not talk about it—unless we can think of a solution to the dilemma."

"I agree. Let us put it aside for now." He lit a candle and quietly began to dress.

Eyes narrowed, Diana gazed at him as he pulled on his breeches. The glow of the candle played along his broad chest and shoulders and on his waist as he bent to pull up the breeches. Diana smiled; she'd been so right. He had great buns!

"Well, I've certainly gotten my mind off our dilemma," she told him.

He bent over and kissed her on top of the head. "I am pleased."

"Do you know what I want?"

He straightened up and grinned at her. "Dare I guess?"

Diana felt herself blush.

"Should I not bother to rebutton my breeches?"

Diana giggled. "That's not what I meant."

"Oh, well, then . . ." He buttoned up.

"*Besides* that," she said, laughing. "I'd really like a Bloody Mary."

"Is that another one of your swear words?"

"No, it's a drink made with tomato juice, gin, pepper, Worcestershire sauce, Tabasco and a sprig of celery."

Adam looked a little confused. "I understood some of that—"

"Never mind." She dropped back down on the bed. "I'll think of an easier drink. I'm sure you have rum in the house."

"Of course. Good Jamaican rum."

"A frozen daiquiri!"

Adam shrugged again.

"And, I think, some stir fry or maybe blackened grouper or . . . scampi?"

"I have no idea what you are talking about, Diana, but we can rouse Mathilde—"

"No, please, not Mathilde." She took his hand. "Come on. Let's go to the kitchen. I'm going to teach you how to make a daiquiri, and then we'll just wing it."

"Wing it?"

"Make it up as we go along, Adam," she said, slipping her arm around his waist. "Just the way we've been doing since I first laid eyes on you."

HALF AN HOUR LATER, they were sitting at the table, sipping drinks Diana had made.

"What do you call this?" Adam asked.

"A daiquiri."

"Interesting." Adam took another long draft and refilled his tankard.

"It's usually sipped."

"I never sip a good drink."

"No, I'm sure you don't. It's easy to make. A little rum, lime juice, sugar. Ice would help. It's meant to be a *frozen* daiquiri." Diana had a sudden mental image of her refrigerator in the Orlando town house. Shining, white, gently humming, with its little window in the door always ready to pour out ice—cubes or crushed. She felt a twinge of sadness for all the twentieth century miracles she might never see again.

"How in the name of the saints could we have ice in the tropics?" Adam seemed genuinely puzzled.

"How, indeed," Diana answered with a sigh. In fact, she had no idea how refrigeration worked. In the old days, there had been ice boxes to keep food cold. But where would they get the ice? "I should have been an engineer," she told Adam. "Then I could explain modern technology and actually prove that I come from another world. Unfortunately, all I know how to do is plug in the cords and turn on the switches. So I can't prove a bloody thing."

"There you go again with your swearing."

"Does it offend you?" she asked.

"Not at all. I find it refreshing."

After drinking half a tankard of daiquiris made with the potent Jamaican rum, Diana abandoned her idea of cooking dinner. Mathilde had left a fish stew warming in a pot on the coals, and Diana found pewter plates and a ladle to dish up the stew. What she couldn't find was a fork.

She rummaged through a drawer of cutlery. "Where are the forks, Adam?"

He sat down at the table, looking content and very much the lord of the manor. "Do you mean those ridiculous foreign utensils with their puny tines?

"Well, yes, that does describe them, I guess."

"A spoon and a knife will do. If necessary we will use God's own utensils—our fingers."

"No forks, then," Diana said, relenting, avoiding the thought of eating with their fingers. She handed him a plate heaped high with fish stew. "Here's a spoon."

She watched him use it to dish up the stew and eat voraciously.

"Well, now," she said. "That seems to work fine." She took a big bite herself. "It holds much more than a fork, in fact." The stew tasted as good as it smelled, redolent with spicy tantalizing flavors. "There's only one thing missing—bread."

Diana got up and began searching the cabinets. "There's bread somewhere, I know it. Aha!" She found half a loaf of freshly baked bread, crusty and firm. "This is one thing we didn't improve in the twentieth century by slicing and packaging," Diana said as she brought the bread to the table. "I bet it'll taste great sopping up the stew."

Adam's grin was disarming. "I never thought that the high-and-mighty spitfire, Lady Diana Tremont, would be moving about barefoot in my kitchen, serving up fish stew and bread."

Diana slipped into a chair across from him, cut herself a big slab of bread and dunked it into the stew. "Don't count on it happening every day. I feel very... very mellow tonight."

"Whatever that feeling is, I pray it continues. It is refreshing."

"Refreshing again?"

"Indeed. I find everything about you refreshing, Diana."

"Even my behavior in town today? You were very angry with me."

"And you with me."

"That's true. I don't like being manhandled. I told you that before."

"You put yourself in danger. I did what I had to do."

Diana sat down at the table beside Adam and met his eyes directly. "What really bothered you, Adam? Were you concerned about my safety—even though I could have won?" she couldn't help reminding him, "or were you afraid I'd escape?"

He didn't answer for a long moment, then he sidestepped the issue. "I am not at all sure you could have won the fight. La Perla is a hellcat out for blood, and she—"

"You aren't answering my question, Adam." Suddenly she started to laugh.

"What amuses you, milady?"

"It's just that nothing has changed through centuries. It's funny, really. Men still equivocate."

"And women?"

"They still put up with it."

"Then I shall answer your question honestly. I was not concerned that you would escape. Even as clever and unpredictable as you are, I knew no one would help you. You are my hostage. And as such, you hold the key to my father's freedom. It was your safety that concerned me this afternoon."

She looked at him with a half smile. "Really?"

"Really. I could not bear for anything to happen to you because..."

"Yes, Adam?"

"Because I am bedazzled and befuddled by you." He reached out and touched her cheek. "Of course you know that, but perhaps you do not know how completely you have affected me."

"I—"

"No, Diana, listen to me for a change. You came into my life like a tempest and knocked me off course. I meant to take you as my hostage—and then I stepped across the bounds of honor and took you to my bed. From one moment to the next, I have not known how to react or what to expect. Will she be playing the role of a madwoman or a temptress—or will she fight in the street like a gypsy?"

"You'll have to wait and see."

Adam threw back his head and laughed. "So. Now you are the temptress again."

"Mercurial," she said.

"Yes, mercurial, for the fleet-footed messenger of the gods."

"Actually, I hadn't thought about it, but of course you're right. The Roman god Mercury," she said.

"And you are surprised that I knew the word?".

"No. Well, I guess so," Diana admitted. "You're a sea captain, after all."

"That does not limit me, Diana."

"I guess not. You're very mercurial yourself. You get angry quickly and then, just as quickly, it's over," she observed.

"As you said, I am a sea captain. I know when a truce is to my advantage." He took her hand.

"And what about La Perla?"

He raised his eyebrows without comment.

"She's very beautiful and so enamored of you that she attacked me with a knife," Diana reminded him.

"Her feelings for me are greatly exaggerated," he said, "and I have no feelings for her. She is nothing like you, Diana. You are fire and ice, mystery and magic." He took her hand and looked deeply into her eyes.

Diana felt like purring with satisfaction, but instead she laughed. "Oh, Adam, this is so crazy! Here we are from two different centuries and I'm feeling happy that you prefer me over someone named La Perla. And I'm thinking about making love to you and spending tomorrow with you. It's all so impossible, you know." She held his hand tightly.

His handsome face became serious, and his eyes darkened with concern. "I know. In time, when you return to your world, I will remain a renegade."

Diana realized that the different worlds Adam was talking about were the worlds of the sea captain and the privileged Lady Diana. He still had no conception of how different their worlds *really* were.

"After that, we may never see each other again," he said.

Diana decided not to mention the real problem, the fact that she belonged in the 1990s. "I understand," she said, wishing that she could also make *him* understand.

"But we have tonight...."

"Yes, a window of opportunity in the great cosmic scheme of things." She pulled away her hand.

"What does that mean, Diana?"

She pushed back from the table, stood up and walked over to the hearth. "A little piece of time, unexpected and unbelievable. How ironic," she said.

Adam came up behind her and slipped his arms around her waist. "I do not understand."

"I know." She paused. "It's funny, really. I've spent so much time worrying about the future, and now I am here in the past—"

"Why not worry about the present then, milady? We will part sooner than we wish, but until then, I will take care of you and protect you." He nuzzled her neck. "And be with you."

With a sigh, she turned in his arms. "Do you have to go to work tomorrow?" At his puzzled look, she explained, "I mean, go aboard ship and see to the crew?"

"Yes, for a while."

"Come home early," she said. "So we can take a day just to be with each other. We'll go to the beach and pack a picnic—"

"Pic-nic?"

Diana laughed aloud. "I'm never sure which words I can use around here. Picnics are...let's see, *al fresco*, cookouts, excursions with food—wine, cheese and bread." She groped for definitions.

"'A loaf of bread, a jug of wine and thou.'"

Diana smiled up at him delightedly. "You know Omar Khayyam!"

"I am a sea captain who also reads—even poetry," he replied a little defensively. "I may not be a peer of the realm, educated at Oxford..."

She touched his cheek with her fingertips. "A most unusual pirate." Diana shook her head in wonder. "I can't believe I'm planning a picnic with an eighteenth-century pirate who can quote eleventh-century poetry—"

"I am not thinking of poetry now. All I am thinking of is spending the day with you on our...pic-nic. Ah, milady, how good it is that we have no barriers between us, no pretenses or fantasies. Life has given us a rare moment."

Diana put her arms around his neck and kissed him long and hard. "Oh, Adam, if you only knew."

8

"IT'S SO BEAUTIFUL!" Diana exclaimed. "So—perfect!"

"You asked me to take you to a perfect spot for a picnic," Adam called out from the back of the boat.

"You're a gem," she cried back.

"Diana, a man cannot be a *jewel*."

"What I mean is— Oh, never mind," Diana said. "I'm getting out." She swung her leg over the side of the boat, grabbed the hem of her skirt and splashed toward shore.

"If you wait, I will—" Adam's words were blown away in the breeze as Diana waded ashore.

The seawater felt like silk against her calves. The beach ahead was a crescent of white sand, as fine as the purest sugar. Palm trees provided shade, and rolling green hills faded gently into the distance. The area was secluded, pristine and very romantic. Diana was charmed and delighted. "I love it, Adam," she cried.

She turned and looked back over her shoulder. Adam had jumped out and was pulling the little sailboat ashore. If she had stayed in her seat, he would have grounded the boat and then offered a hand to help her out. But for once Diana didn't need his help.

Happy to be on her own, she raced through the shallow water onto the dry sand and ran along the beach. Turning in the breeze, laughing, free and happy, Diana looked back toward the sea again.

Adam had pulled the boat completely out of the water and firmly entrenched it in the sand. Diana watched as he lifted out a huge basket, a bottle of wine and a rolled-up rug, which he then balanced on his shoulder. He wobbled a little under the weight, causing Diana to call out.

"Get a move on, Captain!" Not waiting for his reply, she charged through the sand to a grove of palms. Each step in the powdery sand was new and full of adventure. Diana had the feeling of being the first person ever to enter the ring of trees, maybe even the first to run on the sandy beach. She felt like an explorer in a new world.

At the fringes of the palm forest, she stopped and leaned against the nearest tree. Yes, she thought, it was as if no one before her had ever looked out on this beautiful panorama with full sunlight on the blinding white sand. For a moment, she was mesmerized by the scene. Then she turned back toward Adam.

He was lugging the supplies across the sand, moving toward her, but not with the freedom Diana had experienced.

She waved enthusiastically. "I'm over here, Adam. This is a great spot for the picnic."

He trudged along. "So far this pic-nic consists of my working while you race about with a fancy for giving orders," he grumbled.

She made a face at him. "You gave lots of orders on the boat. 'Shorten the jib and hoist the anchor and hard to lee'—whatever that means."

Adam put down the basket and unrolled the rug. "I was teaching you to sail, woman. You said you wanted to learn."

"I did—and I do. But I can only absorb a little at a time." Diana turned again in the salty sea breeze and spread her arms toward the heavens. The sun beat down on her face, and the breeze ruffled her hair. "What a day! I know how Robinson Crusoe must have felt on his perfect island where no other person had ever trod."

"I am afraid a few have trod here," Adam said as he dropped the supplies in the sand beside her.

"Who?"

"My sailors. I have been here myself," he told her.

"Alone—or with La Perla?"

"Alone."

"I don't believe you. But never mind. No matter whose footprints were made in the sand, I'm not the first intruder. Do you suppose there's a beach where no one has ever set foot?"

"Possibly." He sank onto the sand. "But you will have to take the boat out and find it yourself, Diana. I am remaining here."

She dropped down beside him. "And I'll remain here with you, happily."

"You seem pleased about everything, milady. Do these pic-nics always cause such joy?"

"Not always. Just under certain conditions." Diana lay back on his lap and gazed up at him. He looked every inch the sailor, with his light growth of beard and windblown hair. His shirt had become unbuttoned, and the muscles of his chest gleamed golden bronze in the sunlight. In another century—her century—Diana would have suspected that he'd unbuttoned the shirt himself, for effect. She had no such suspicions here in 1724. Besides the white shirt, he wore baggy white trousers that reached just below the knees, and no shoes. That was hardly the outfit of a macho twentieth-century male.

"And furthermore, Captain," Diana said, continuing to answer his question, "I've decided to take your advice."

He settled closer to her on the sand and gave a quizzical look.

"You advised me to live in the present."

"Ah, so I did. And not worry about the past—"

"Or the future," she reminded him. That's what I'm doing today, and I'm having a fabulous time."

"Fabulous," he repeated.

Diana laughed. "Do you know what I mean?" She wasn't sure whether she'd chosen a word of her time or his.

"Yes. You mean exceptional." He smoothed back a windblown wisp of her hair. "Like yourself."

"And you," she said, smiling into his eyes. He had unusual eyes, she noticed, not dark brown as she'd once thought, but in the sun they seemed more golden in color, with flecks of green. He smiled down at her, and she touched the lines around his eyes. She'd learned that her Adam was a man with a great zest for life, a man who enjoyed every moment to the fullest. She could learn from him.

"We're going to be totally alone here, aren't we?" she asked. "No villagers or crew members turning up?"

"Hmm." He ran his finger lightly across her lips. "Now, I wonder why you ask that, milady?"

Diana felt herself blushing unaccountably. "Just curious," she said with a smile.

"We are alone. My crew is occupied elsewhere."

"Living it up at the Blood and Guts?"

"Blood and Bones," he said, correcting her. "In fact, they are hard at work careening the *Black Hawke* on the leeward side of the island."

"Careening? That sounds dangerous."

"Not at all. It simply means the ship has been run aground and turned on her side for scraping."

"Without the captain there to supervise?"

"Russell will see that everything is done well. The man is my right arm."

"It's great to have such a friend."

"I trust him with my ship. He will supervise the crew as they scrape and clean the ship's bottom and then smear it with tar and tallow. The ocean takes a fearsome toll on a seagoing vessel."

"Especially a wooden one," Diana commented.

"What other kind would there be?" he asked.

"Someday there might be ships built of other materials," she said.

"Hmm, I cannot imagine that. In any case, this one will be seaworthy again soon."

"Soon? Does that mean you plan another voyage?" The voyage to trade her to Sir Winston for Adam's father, Diana thought nervously.

He met her gaze directly. "Not soon at all, milady. Tarring a ship the size of the *Black Hawke* will take a while. There is no hurry."

He seemed relaxed, and Diana wished her own anxiety could be so easily dispelled, but she had to ask the inevitable question. "Is there any word from my... from Sir Winston?"

"By now he has my letter of demands and will act soon. Whatever else he is, Grenville is a man of quick decision. But you know that."

"I don't know anything about him!" Diana protested.

Adam raised an eyebrow quizzically.

"I really don't," she repeated.

He took her hand. "Compose yourself, Diana. Do not let Grenville ruin our time together. Such a glorious day as this may never come again."

His calmness seemed to flow into her.

Diana took a deep breath and willed herself to relax. Adam was right; there was nothing she could do but follow his advice and live for the present. And wait. And hope.

"Now it is your turn to teach me, milady," he teased, steering the subject far away from the *Black Hawke* and Grenville. "About this pic-nic. When do we eat the vittles that Mathilde prepared for us?"

She pretended to think. "After."

"After? That sounds intriguing. After what, I wonder." He cocked his eyebrow. "After we . . ."

"After we swim," she said, finishing for him.

"Not possible," he said flatly. "Women do not swim, especially ladies. And neither do men—unless their boat has sunk and they are paddling for their lives."

"Paddling? I'll bet that's what you do! A dog paddle of some kind." Diana caught herself at the beginning of a self-satisfied smirk. Here was something from her era that she could actually introduce to Adam. The Australian crawl, which she'd learned at her first swimming lessons when she was seven years old, hadn't appeared in the West until the twentieth century. If she could tempt Adam into a contest she could probably win. Now, that might be fun! Even a pirate captain needed a comeuppance now and then. "Want to race?" she asked.

"A foot race?"

"Nope. A swimming race. From, let's say, the beach here to that point of land at the end of the cove." Diana wasn't sure she could make it that far without getting severely winded, but her crawl and strong kick had to be faster than whatever kind of stroke Adam might know.

"I have never seen a lady swim," Adam said in amazement. "Although I have heard tell that in the South Sea islands women do go into the water. Of course, we all know that islanders are part fish."

"Well, I do swim, and I'm not part fish," Diana announced. "I even have a swimsuit."

"What is that?"

"Oh, of course. A bathing costume. It's called a swimsuit, and I whipped one up just for our little outing."

Suddenly she was very nervous. It had seemed amusing this morning to wheedle cloth, scarves, needle and thread out of Mathilde to put together something resembling a swimsuit. Now, in the bright glare of the sun, which revealed a multitude of imperfections, she was hesitant about taking off the familiar skirt and blouse to parade around in the 'bathing costume' that closely resembled a bikini.

Adam threw back his head and laughed. "A bathing costume! Sweet Jesu, woman, why would you need a costume for bathing? Surely the best one would be what God has given you. When you take a bath, you do not cover yourself, do you?"

"You have a point, Adam, but it's different outside on the beach. When we go swimming or sunbathing, there're usually other people around, and so we—"

"Who is this 'we'?" he asked suspiciously.

"Oh, people like me," she said lamely. "People of my—"

"Yes?"

Diana had almost said 'time,' but changed her mind at the last moment. "People of my . . . kind. We put on bathing suits and take picnic lunches and go to the beach to swim and play volleyball—"

"The Tremonts are certainly different," he observed. "A most eccentric family. Well, then, let me see this bathing costume of yours."

"I have it on under my clothes."

He raised one eyebrow.

"I—I made it myself." Diana got to her feet, aware that it was too late to back out now but unsure of her next step. Should she take off the blouse or the skirt first?

"Well, then, let me see," he repeated.

Diana's modesty seemed foolish. After all, she and Adam had spent hours in bed, engaged in every sort of intimate act. Yet she always seemed to blush under his gaze, and she felt suddenly shy to stand in front of him in the bright sunlight to model a homemade swimsuit.

She moved a few steps away, and he followed her with his eyes.

"Adam—"

"I am waiting."

"Okay." She took a deep breath, then turned away to pull off her blouse and step out of her skirt. Remembering to stand up straight and pull in her tummy, she turned back toward him and asked, "Well, what do you think?"

"Holy Mother of God..." Adam got to his feet and began to walk around her, like a wolf circling its prey. "You would wear this in public?"

"Well, yes . . ."

"In front of other people?"

She nodded.

"In front of men?"

Diana looked down at her 'bikini.' She'd used one scarf for the top, knotted it in the middle and tied the ends around her neck. Admittedly the material was thin and showed the outline of her breasts and nipples, but at least she was covered. For the bikini bottom, she'd tied two other scarves together and knotted them on either side of her hips. The result was a covering that rode suggestively low and revealed, she suspected, a little more than what was necessary of her behind. She looked around but couldn't be sure what was exposed, so she tugged a little. That didn't seem to help, and Adam was still staring, waiting for an answer.

"Actually," she began hesitantly, "women wear these all the time."

He shook his head in disbelief.

"They do," she said, defending herself. "At Daytona and Fort Lauderdale and . . ." Her voice trailed off. Adam had no idea what she was talking about.

"Have you ever shown yourself in such a bathing suit as this in public, before other men?" He planted himself squarely in front of her, and his face was clouded with doubt and confusion.

Diana thought quickly. She hadn't taken into account that Adam might be shocked by her outfit—and even jealous. For all his boldness and daring, he was a man of his time. But Diana had an answer for him.

"In a bathing suit made of scarves? No, never."

He smiled and the cloud of doubt disappeared. "'Tis good my crew is on the far side of the island, for I would kill any man who saw you abroad in the daylight like this."

"Surely not kill them."

"Yes, just as I said. You are a precious sight, but for my eyes alone."

And lurking in his eyes was a burning flame of desire, which warmed her more than the heat from the sun.

"Yes," he said, "a very lovely sight."

Adam ran his fingers down her neck to her collarbone and then along the top of her makeshift suit. Her skin tingled not just where he touched her but in anticipation of the spot he would touch next.

"I have a fancy for this swim—suit?"

"Yes, suit," she echoed.

"You must wear it *only* for me." He moved his hand to her waist and lower along her hip, caressing the roundness of her bottom through the scarf.

"Only for you, Adam." Diana let her hand drift, too, across his chest, absorbing his warmth as she moved her fingers through the sprinkling of soft hairs. The sun beat down on her back, adding its rays to the heat between them. Only the soft breeze in the palms could prevent that heat from turning to fire.

Diana felt the heat in Adam's kiss as he pulled her close. His lips were hard and demanding. And she felt it in his skin, moist against her. She kissed him back, mouth open, her tongue seeking his.

They dropped to their knees and rolled over onto the rug, locked in each other's arms. All thoughts of the picnic were banished from Diana's mind. The blazing sun was no hotter than the fire of desire that she felt inside.

Adam fumbled with the scarf that she'd knotted in the front, untied it and freed her breasts to his hands and mouth. She gave a convulsive shudder of pleasure. This was their own paradise, where another of her fantasies was about to be played out, the one in which she made love to her handsome pirate on the beach. Was every fantasy she'd imagined destined to come true?

Diana had no time to wonder, for now Adam was untying the knot at her hips and pulling away the scarves. His tongue caressed her in all the secret places that gave her joy, and she felt the heat penetrate her skin and invade her very being.

Diana lay back on the rug and let him kiss her, taste her, lick her, while she sank deeper into her fantasy. "If only this could go on forever," she murmured. "And yet—"

"And yet?" he asked, lifting his head to look at her.

"It's my turn to—" she reached out and tugged at his shirt "—undress you." She pulled off the shirt, then rolled on her side and unbuttoned his breeches. "Lift up a little," she advised, and he lifted his hips. She pulled the breeches down his legs, uncovering him inch by inch. First his strong muscular thighs, then his hard, bronzed calves.

"You're so beautiful," she whispered.

He laughed softly. "A man cannot be beautiful."

"You are."

His skin smelled like the fresh air and tasted of the salty sea. She licked his chin, his throat and collarbone and then slid her lips to the hardness of his taut nipples. She felt him tense beneath her as she flicked the tight buds with her tongue.

"I hope this pleases you, my darling," she murmured, "as much as you please me."

Diana ran her tongue teasingly along his hipbone, and Adam groaned at her touch, causing her lips to curve in a satisfied smile. She let her lips wander lower and she tasted his manhood. It, too, was hot, like the rest of his body and hers. She used her tongue and mouth to make him grow and harden, until Adam cried out, "No more, no more. Would you drive me mad?"

She understood that cry, for her own desire was building as fast as his—an aching tightness that spiraled within her. Adam cupped her breasts with his hands, and the pressure of his palm against her swollen nipple caused Diana to moan with desire. The tightness inside her twisted and knotted and begged for release.

She slid over onto Adam's hips, one knee on each side of him, then she lifted and guided his erection into her welcoming moistness. Every sensation she felt was magnified a thousand times—the hard length of him filling her, the tightness, the friction and the heat, always the heat.

Every cell of her body pulsed with awareness, and her own need glowed inside as fiercely as the sun. She gazed down at her lover. His eyes met hers, transfixed with a look of rapture. There was a primitive wildness in their lovemaking, a power that was almost primeval. Diana threw back her head and held on to his shoulder tightly as Adam lifted his hips toward her, and they were joined in the rhythm of love.

"There is no woman like you, Diana," Adam whispered afterwards. "I have never known such joy with another."

"I know," Diana said, kissing him softly, her words blurred against his mouth. "It's as though you and I were somehow meant to be—"

Meant to be! Dear God, she thought, *is that what has happened? Somehow Adam and I are meant to be, joined across time and space, against all reason and logic?*

She looked at him, lying beside her, sated with lovemaking, one arm possessively touching her hip. Wonderingly Diana shook her head. What was happening to her? Suddenly, clearly, she knew. She was falling in love.

JUST BEFORE TWILIGHT time, Adam lit a fire. Neither he nor Diana was anxious to leave the tranquillity of the beach. She sat across from him, her back against a palm tree. She'd found a comfortable spot nestled between the oval-shaped slabs of bark, and she was sketching with the charcoal tip of a burned sliver of wood.

"What are you drawing so avidly in Mr. Defoe's book?" Adam asked.

"I'm not drawing in the book," she assured him. "A blank page at the back came loose so I decided to use it as sketch paper."

"Hmm." Adam had put his shirt and breeches on and was lounging on the rug, drinking from a tankard of wine. The firelight cast shadows across his face and highlighted his strong features—the square chin, straight nose and the hollows below his cheekbones. Diana found herself staring, fascinated. She was struck by the feeling that she and Adam might be a man and woman from any time, together on their own private beach. It was reassuring—two lovers enjoying the day and each other with no thought of the world outside.

"But what is the subject of your drawing?" he asked.

"It's almost too dark to see." Diana passed the book to him. "A sketch of you. Just rough, but—"

Adam looked with amazement at the sketch, studying it carefully before looking back at her. "You made this drawing yourself?"

"Yes, Adam, of course."

"It hardly seems possible. A woman, drawing so quickly, and such a good likeness."

"A woman?"

"Yes, I have not heard tell of a woman artist."

"You'd be surprised," she said.

"I am surprised—and impressed."

"It would be much better if I had real drawing pencils instead of this homemade charcoal. I love to draw," she told him.

"Is that how you amuse yourself back in England?"

"Hardly amusement, Adam. I am—I was," she said, correcting herself, "a working woman. In Orlando, not England. I designed clothes and had my own shop."

"The Tremonts allowed their kin to engage in trade! This village of Orlando must be quite strange. I believe you are telling me tall tales again for your amusement."

"One of my little fantasies, my creative stories about coming from the twentieth century?" she asked mockingly.

"You must admit, Diana, that you are a very imaginative woman," Adam said seriously. "You have told fantastical tales—" he smiled proudly "fabulous tales—from the very beginning. Sometimes I think you believe them yourself."

Diana took a deep breath, settled more comfortably against the bark of the tree and decided to try again. She and Adam were both relaxed; the afternoon had brought them closer, not only physically but emotionally. Maybe, just maybe, this was the right time to make him listen seriously.

She spoke with great care. "I know you don't believe me, Adam, and I don't blame you. I'm sure what I've been telling you sounds farfetched and crazy. If you had appeared in the twentieth century with the explanation that you had somehow come to my world from 1724, I would think you needed to be committed."

Adam listened to her with the serious expression she'd hoped for, but it was mixed with a real puzzlement.

"All right. I don't belong in this century. I'm from the future. Oh, damn. That sounds absurd. There's just no way to explain," she said in frustration.

He remained quiet, watching her carefully. She certainly had his attention, Diana realized. She clenched her fists, closed her eyes and started again.

"I want to convince you, but there's nothing I can do, because my talents are so limited. I could tell you that people draw pictures on computers, but what good would that do? You have no idea what a computer is."

"Right you are, Diana."

She laughed. "That sounds so modern. It's amazing how some expressions have lasted for hundreds of years. Too bad it can't work backward so you'd understand the word 'computer.'" She groaned. "Oh, *why* didn't I study to be an engineer—or a scientist? All I can do is draw pictures and make a daiquiri! I'm afraid that's not going to convince you that I really live—or lived—in the 1990s."

Adam sat up, a worried frown still creasing his brow. "I think, milady, that this *is* true—"

Diana leaned toward him. "You do?"

"It is true for you—in your mind. You have told these stories so often that they have become real."

"Oh, Adam, you even understand psychiatry!"

"I may understand it, but I do not know what it is."

Diana laughed aloud. "I never dreamed my pirate would have a sense of humor. And you know what? You may just be right about my stories. Maybe all this *is* in my imagination."

"Of course it is. You are remarkably imaginative—and creative. I learn that each time we make love." He smiled. "Today you were especially inventive."

Diana sank back against the tree. "I'm not talking about sex, Adam. That's universal, timeless. What I want you to understand—and what I'm trying to understand myself—is that as imaginative as I am, I couldn't have thought this all up. I just couldn't have," Diana repeated to convince herself. "I'm totally out of place here." She looked around at the deep purple colors of the sunset on the sea. "Oh, not here, not on this beach with you. . . ."

"No, you belong here. We belong here together. It has been a day to remember," Adam said.

"Yes, it has been that, but I'm still obsessed with the *how* and *why* of it all. I understand there are people who claim to have lived in the past, who have had other lives and been reincarnated. I never believed them, but maybe it is possible. But it doesn't work the other way around. Nobody claims to have lived in the future and come back to tell about it. Except in movies. And this is no movie. And I'm *more* than just an imaginative woman of the 1700s. I'm Diana Tremont, from Orlando, Florida, dammit, and I live in another time."

She glanced at him. His expression had changed to one of polite, but strained, interest and poorly hidden incredulity.

"If I could just tell you the things that are going to happen in the next two hundred and seventy years. . . ."

"Women in trade, wearing bathing costumes?" he asked jokingly.

"That and much more. The colonies will revolt against England—"

"It takes no prophet to predict that," he interrupted. "The tyrant George will fall in time, as everyone knows. It will happen."

"It's already happened, Adam. I mean— Oh, hell, what do I mean? In about fifty more years, the flames of freedom will sweep across the world—first the colonies, then Europe and Russia. New countries will form and old ones will divide or disappear." Diana laughed at herself. "I sound like a history book."

"You speak with such conviction, Diana."

"Oh, the tales I could tell, of ships that fly in the sky, men who have traveled to the moon!"

Adam laughed and held out his arms. "Come here, to me, my Scheherazade. You have more than a thousand and one tales. I shall see that you have paper and pen so that you can write them all down."

Diana moved away from the tree to sit beside him and lean her head against his shoulder. "No," she said softly, "I'll keep my tales just for you."

The moon was rising above the distant hills, and they gazed at it through the lacy tracings of the palm fronds. It really didn't matter, what she knew about the future, Diana thought. There was nothing she could do about it. Adam was right. What counted now was the present—his arms around her, the moon shining down on them, the flickering light of the fire.

He kissed her softly on the forehead and tightened his arms around her. The moment was blissful, perfect. Diana closed her eyes and sighed. There was no doubt about what she was feeling. As strange as her life had become, one thing proved true. She was in love with Adam Hawke. How could she not love him when he was everything she'd ever wanted in a man?

It was all impossible, of course. She would still be shipped away from Adam in trade for his father. Even though he no longer spoke of it, she was sure Adam hadn't forgotten the trade for a moment. She also knew he would never back down on his pledge to free Simon Hawke. Diana shivered with dread, which Adam mistook for a chill.

"It is cold here in the night air, milady. Let me take you home to the warmth of our bed."

She nodded and helped put out the fire and pack up their belongings. Diana was quiet on the trip back to the village. Loving Adam was something she hadn't counted on. The feeling made her head swim with joy and her body tremble with anticipation. She'd never been in love before, and the feeling was overpowering. But if she knew anything at all, Diana knew that it was also going to make her life much more complicated.

9

A FEW DAYS LATER, Diana puttered around the kitchen of Adam's house.

"*What*, I wonder," she mused, "can I substitute for soy sauce?"

"I can in no wise tell what ye be talkin' about, ladyship."

Mathilde was wearing the same tight expression of disapproval that came over her face every time Diana entered her kitchen.

"Maybe vinegar!" Diana decided excitedly.

Mathilde made a point of clattering the pewter bowls as she put them on the shelf, without responding to Diana's exclamation.

"I've used vinegar in stir-fry," Diana mused, "but in what proportions? And how? If I could only remember. First I wished I'd been an engineer. Now I wish I'd been a cook." She turned around and spoke directly to Mathilde. "I was always too busy to cook."

Mathilde made a low clucking noise that indicated her disapproval. "The cap'n won't be likin' this," she warned, "unless I'm very mistook."

"How do you know? I haven't even started yet," Diana said, "because I'm missing ingredients. What about cooking oil? I don't suppose there's a low-fat polyunsaturated vegetable oil around here? Maybe I can make do with this awful looking stuff that's made from beef fat."

Mathilde clucked again.

"I suppose it's what we call lard. It should work in a wok or whatever will pass for a wok. I'll stir in these vegetables and make a dish your captain will love. With a few spices thrown in," she added.

"Don't ye be meddlin' for spices in my cabinets, ladyship," she ordered.

"How could I, when you're watching over me like a hawk?"

"Exceptin' that just now I'll be leavin' you alone—"

"Oh?" Diana's eyes lit up.

"So to see to those lazy wenches in the wash room. I give 'em orders to boil the linens and they spend the time gossipin'." She paused at the door.

"I won't be meddlin' in your spices," Diana said, smiling innocently.

As soon as she was alone, Diana made a beeline for the spice cabinet, opened the door and peered in. It was filled with little bottles and jars, unlabeled and very peculiar looking. When she took the lids off, strange aromas assailed her.

"Ugh." She wrinkled her nose. One jar smelled like dead fish, and another like stale tobacco. She rummaged further and found a jar of ginger and a string of red chili peppers.

Diana took them back to the work table and slumped into a chair. Her plan was to produce a healthful Chinese stir-fry, but she was having trouble remembering the recipe, and substituting these makeshift ingredients for the ones she did remember could be disastrous.

She sighed loudly. It was funny what she missed from her own time—little things like soy sauce for her cooking. What else? Safety pins. Moisturizer. Ice cubes. But there were some things she could do without—like television and radio. It was refreshing not to have talking heads blaring bad news twenty-four hours a day. She didn't miss newspapers, either, although now and then she longed for a good crossword puzzle.

Cars, buses, airplanes—she didn't miss them, either. She and Adam had walked from the house to town along the path bordered by plants and flowers that bloomed in profusion with no help from chemical fertilizers and insect sprays. The air around them was clear and cloudless, free of pollution, and the sea was pure and crystal clear.

In many ways life on Rogue's Cay was very pleasant. All of Diana's creature comforts were taken care of. Mathilde kept a houseful of servants working from dawn to dusk. Pots of hot water were available for bathing, and there was certainly no danger of starving. Bananas, mangoes and guavas were plentiful, and the old lady did have a talent for baking bread.

But Diana missed her family and her friends at Fantasy Faire. She knew they must be concerned about her—if they knew her circumstances they'd worry even more. Adam's spies had returned with the news that Sir Winston, after an angry tirade against traitorous colonials, had agreed to Adam's terms. She was to be traded, but she didn't know where or when.

At a loss about how to extricate herself from 1724, Diana was making the most of her life on Rogue's Cay. She had books now, walks on the beach and sailing lessons. And at night there was Adam. She made a deliberate effort each day to concentrate on the here and now, enjoy the beauty of her surroundings and her time with Adam. If she'd learned nothing else from her bizarre entrapment in the eighteenth century, it was that only the moment counted, and it should be enjoyed to the fullest.

She would begin by enjoying a good meal for a change. Mathilde's reliance on fish stew, salted beef and stringy goat meat left much to be desired. Diana had gone back to rummaging through the ingredient possibilities, when she heard a commotion in the courtyard. Thinking Adam had returned from town early, she went to the door.

Several men were gathered in the far corner of the courtyard, shouting loudly. She recognized a few obscenities but most of the rest was gibberish. The men seemed to be struggling, and one had fallen. The others gathered around him, and the shouting intensified. Diana looked around, thinking she should call for help, when Adam appeared at the gate.

"Adam, there's a fight—"

"Get back into the kitchen, Diana," he ordered.

"But Adam—"

"I will handle it."

She nodded and stepped back into the doorway but didn't go inside immediately. Instead she watched him cross the courtyard toward the battling men. For a moment she thought of staying to see the outcome, but decided against it. Adam was right. They were his men and his problem. She had no cause to interfere.

Diana went into the kitchen and closed the door behind her, intent upon her own problem—creating a dinner that both she and Adam would enjoy.

"I know Mathilde has garlic in here somewhere," she muttered. Suddenly Mathilde burst into the kitchen, moving faster than Diana thought possible.

"Oh, my God, lady, they're crazed notions he has, my cap'n."

"What are you talking about, Mathilde?"

"He won't be crossed, and there's the truth of it."

"Mathilde, talk sense, please."

"The cap'n's gone mad. Oh, sweet Jesu!"

"Mad? The captain—" Diana didn't try to decipher Mathilde's ravings but rushed back to the courtyard, her heart pounding. The old woman was behind her, crying furiously.

Diana flung open the door and stepped onto the cobblestones. All was quiet; there wasn't a sound of fighting, and the men had disappeared. Except for one. He was tied to a post in the middle of the courtyard. A few feet away, Adam stood, a black whip in his hand.

Diana called out to Adam. "What are you doing? Stop!" She moved forward, but his voice froze her in midstep.

"Get back in the kitchen now, woman. This is none of your affair. Take her away, Mathilde."

Mathilde tugged at Diana's blouse, but Diana didn't budge.

"You go," she told the old woman. "I'm staying."

Without another word, Mathilde ducked back inside the doorway and from there motioned for Diana to come, too.

"Close the door," Diana said.

In the middle of the courtyard, Adam watched and waited. The door closed; Diana stood her ground.

Adam's face was clouded, and angrier than Diana had ever seen it.

"I am dealing with a traitor among my men," he said. "This is our way of punishing traitors. It has nothing to do with you."

"I can't stand by and watch a man be whipped!"

"Then go inside as I suggested."

"It's cruel and unnecessary punishment," she said.

"You are talking nonsense again, woman. It is the punishment for men of the sea. It has been thus for many a year and it will remain thus."

Diana started to respond, but was suddenly out of words. She was an intruder in this courtyard—and in this world. Maybe he was right; maybe she should obey his orders and leave the punishment to him.

She stepped back and was reaching behind her for the knob of the door, when the man strapped to the post cried out in a shaking voice, "I be innocent, your ladyship. I would never do naught to harm ye."

"Russell," she cried. "It's Russell!"

"I would never disobey my cap'n—"

Diana held her ground. If Russell was telling the truth, everything was different now. She called out to Adam again. "Russell is your friend. You've trusted him with your ship and your life, and now you're going to beat him? Why, Adam, why?"

"Russell is a traitor, and I intend to deal with him as a traitor. I warn you one more time, leave this to me."

Diana's knees and legs felt wobbly and her throat dry, but she wasn't going to slink away and leave Russell to be whipped like a dog. "What is it, Russell?" she called out. "If Adam won't tell me—"

"I never had naught plan to take you off the island, lady. Pay no heed to what La Perla says. I own I'm innocent—"

"A plan to kidnap me?" Fearless now, Diana surged forward to stand just a few feet from Adam. "Surely you don't believe this."

Adam's voice was tight; his words low and cold. "I have it on good authority that La Perla and Russell plotted to kidnap you and deal with Sir Winston on their own. They planned to trade you for gold and leave my father to die in that hellhole of a prison." Adam's face was twisted with dark rage and pain. "Russell must be punished for such an act."

"If it were true, yes, he should be punished. But it's not true. It can't be. And I'm astounded that you'd listen to gossip like that." She inched closer. "It's just foolish talk with no facts to back it up. You're...you're acting like a tyrant!"

The slight waver in his eyes encouraged Diana to go on. She threw his own words back in his face. "Aren't you always blathering on about the British and how tyrannical they are to the colonists, about how there's no fair hearing under the law? Now you're acting worse. Much worse."

The cold look in Adam's eyes didn't waver. "By thunder, woman, I shall decide how to discipline my own men."

"Discipline? This isn't discipline. This is cruelty of the first order, and if I know anything, I know you aren't a cruel man. What's come over you, Adam? You haven't even listened to Russell's side of the story."

"Are you saying I cannot run my own ship? Are you saying I do not know how to handle my men?"

Diana took a deep breath. At least he was talking to her. She ventured to put her hand on his arm. "I'm not saying that, but there are important principles at stake here like—like—innocent until proven guilty and due process and a man's entitlement to a trial before a jury of his peers."

Looking at her in amazement, Adam shook her hand away. "Your words make no sense, lady. They are just high-flown rhetoric."

Diana's shoulders sagged. Of course Adam had no idea what she was talking about. The Constitution of the United States and the Bill of Rights were more than sixty years into the future.

She had one last chance. "You're doing to Russell just what Sir Winston and his cohorts did to you. You're taking away a man's rights arbitrarily, you're not listening to his side and you're acting like a dictator. Russell is being sentenced without a trial when you could be wrong, Adam." She moved in front of him, between Russell and the whip. "You could be punishing an innocent man."

"Move aside, lady. I would not want to hurt you." Adam looped the whip around his hand.

"Oh, for God's sake, Adam, what if you're wrong? What if you punish this man, who's your friend, unjustly? That makes you no better than those who drove you away from your home. It makes you no better than the men you claim to hate so vehemently. If you whip Russell, you sink to their level."

Adam wavered. Diana held her ground. Their eyes met and locked.

Everything was quiet in the courtyard. The birds that had been singing were stilled, the activities of the house came to a halt and even the breeze seemed to have stopped.

With a curse, Adam threw the whip to the ground. Diana felt her body sag with relief as he called out to the sailors who'd been standing in the shadows.

"Unchain this man and return him to his cell in the village."

"No, Adam—"

The look he gave her silenced Diana immediately. There was only so much she could expect from him.

"I will question him later," Adam told the men. "Round up any man who would come forward as a witness."

A grateful and shaken Russell was led away. "I thank ye, your ladyship," he mumbled, "I thank ye." As he departed he called over his shoulder to Adam, "By your leave, Cap'n, I own I'm innocent, and to say truth, 'tis only rumors started by that witch of a woman—"

"Let that suffice for now," Adam said, waving him away.

When the men were gone and the courtyard was empty again, Adam addressed Diana coolly. "Are you satisfied, milady?"

She should have taken a step back, lowered her eyes and nodded affirmatively. If she'd been an eighteenth-century woman she might have done just that, but Diana couldn't help transcending time and making her thoughts known—again. "You're angry now because you know I'm right. You weren't behaving like the Adam I know. You were behaving like a barbarian."

His laugh was more like a snicker. "Perhaps I am a barbarian, lady."

"No—"

"Yes. You might wish to call me a gentleman of fortune, but it is high time you faced the truth. I live by my wits and strength. I control a band of cutthroats and criminals."

"No, no. You're wrong, Adam. You're not the kind of man to rule by terror and fear like Blackbeard or Captain Kidd. Beating an innocent man would have been despicable. Your men would never have respected you for such behavior, but they will respect a strong man, a man of honor. That's what you are. I know that. And I know you. You never would hurt Russell." Her voice broke.

Adam grasped her arm with his strong fingers. "You do not know me, lady," he said. "I told you that once before, and still you do not believe me."

"Yes, I do! You're a man of honor, and I trust you. Come with me into the house. We can talk—"

Adam's face was hard and his words icy. "I have had enough of your talk for now, Lady Diana. This eighteenth-century pirate will take himself from your sight. I have no idea when I shall return."

He kicked the whip out of his path and strode from the courtyard, head high, shoulders tight with anger.

Tears blurred Diana's eyes as she watched him go. How clear their differences were. He was, as he'd told her, not a gentleman of fortune but an outlaw and rebel. The captain of a pirate ship.

Diana moved slowly across the courtyard back toward the kitchen, where she'd left Mathilde. She'd learned so much today, that Adam was a prisoner of his time just as she was of hers. All they'd had together were just stolen moments. And perhaps there wouldn't be many more of those.

Oh, she'd won a small battle, but she never would win the war. Although she loved Adam, her love wasn't enough. She couldn't change him or the world he lived in any more than she could control her own destiny, which was unwinding so rapidly before her.

TRUE TO HIS word, Adam didn't come home that night. The sky darkened and clouds rolled in from the west, burying the moon in its blackness. The thunder that rumbled in the distance grew closer as night approached, and Diana's feelings became as dark as the inky sky.

As the night descended, Diana went out onto the balcony, unmindful of the wind or the light haze of rain against her face. Even though her confrontation with Adam had been terrible in its intensity, she was glad it had happened. It had brought everything clearly into focus.

Diana leaned against the balcony rail, wondering if she needed to be hit on the head by another tree limb to realize that she was living in a dream. No matter how real the events in the courtyard, all this still remained as her fantasy.

"A dream," she muttered. "A figment of both our imaginations, Adam's and mine. He'll never behave like a man from my time, and I can never live here."

Yet, what was her option? If she didn't return to her own time, she'd be sent away to a godfather she'd never seen.

A noise behind her startled Diana, and she turned, hoping to see Adam. But it was Mathilde, her old face etched with lines of concern and worry.

"It warn't my intention to afright you, lady."

"It's all right, Mathilde," Diana said.

"Let me fetch you in, away from the thunder and lightning that's aragin' out here. Sich can be dangerous, lady."

"Don't I know it," Diana muttered. "Lightning got me into this mess."

"Ye best come inside and have some vittles."

"I'm not hungry," Diana said stubbornly.

"It's time you supped, and I'll make ye a cup of tea. Would ye be likin' that?"

Diana pushed her windblown hair away from her face. The old lady was trying to be kind and make an overture of friendship for the first time. Now, somehow, they were in this together, and Diana valued the sudden friendship. "Yes please, Mathilde, and some of your bread. I think we'll be eating alone tonight."

THE STORM WORSENED. Thunder rolled across the sea in earnest and blasted open the heavens. Lightning blazed, and the rain came down in torrents. Diana threw open the shutters to her room and let the elements surround her.

She didn't fear the storm; she relished it. The torrential downpour was no different from the one she'd been caught in on that fateful night. No matter the era, the heavens erupted in a similar explosive way. She was reminded of her other life, and she wanted it back again.

Lifting her face to the stinging rain, Diana prayed aloud, "I want to go home!"

A blinding flash of light and an earthshaking peal of thunder were the only answers to her prayer.

The Lord helps those who help themselves. She'd heard that saying a hundred times, and suddenly it took on real meaning for Diana. More thunder shook the sky, reinforcing her sudden decision. She turned from the window, feeling freed at last, and bolted from the room.

Charging down the stairs, she ran headlong into Mathilde, whom she had to hold up so the old woman wouldn't crash to the floor.

"Lady, lady, in the name of heaven, where be ye goin' on a night like this?"

"Home," Diana shouted as she opened the door. It caught on the wind and blew wildly back and forth. "Home!"

Mathilde's pleas and imprecations were lost in the crack of lightning and roar of wind. Buffeted by the storm, her dress soaked and clinging to her, Diana fought her way up the bluff above the house.

By now the rain had so completely soaked the hillside that it seemed to be giving way under her. She clutched for vines and shrubs and climbed on, determined to reach her goal. The thunder and lightning crashed all around; she ignored them.

Clawing in the mud, she finally reached the top of the cliff and stood straight, in spite of the roaring storm. The wind whipped through her hair. The cold rain beat against her. It didn't matter; none of that mattered. Her clothes clung wetly to her, and she didn't care.

Diana held her arms up to the sky. "I want to go home," she shouted again.

A jagged streak of lightning tore through the black night. Diana shut her eyes and waited. The crash of thunder that followed was the loudest she'd ever heard. It seemed to shake the very ground beneath her.

She stood, swaying in the wind, waiting, her eyes still tightly closed.

After a long while, she opened her eyes. To her dismay, nothing had changed. She was still on the same cliff, in the same century.

"I want to go home," she shouted again, moving closer to the edge of the cliff. Her need to have the prayer answered was far greater than her fear of falling into the abyss. She took another step and looked down to the sea, which roared violently below. Updrafts of wind buffeted her and made it difficult for her to stand upright.

She fought for solid footing, but the rain had loosened the sand and gravel at the rim of the bluff. Another blaze of lightning shot through the night air, and unsteadily, she lifted her arms to the sky and boldly took another step forward. The earth seemed to give way beneath her foot.

Wind and darkness engulfed her as Diana waved her arms wildly fighting for balance. But there was nothing there for her to cling to. All was darkness.

Then strong arms grabbed her and pulled her away from the edge.

"No, Diana, my love, no. This is not the answer—"

He enfolded her in his arms, and she opened her eyes to look up at him. Rain poured down Adam's face, his wet hair stuck to his forehead and his shirt was molded to his body. His dark cloak blew wildly in the wind.

"It's all right, Adam," she shouted against the wind. "I wasn't going to throw myself over the cliff. I was just trying to go home."

Adam pulled off his cloak and wrapped her in it. "I shall take you home, Diana. Home with me." He enclosed her in his arms and started down the hill, leading her gently and carefully.

ONCE IN THE HOUSE, Adam took charge of a shivering Diana. Too tired to argue, she did as she was told without protests.

"Drink this," Adam ordered. "It is a rum toddy."

Diana took a sip from the steaming tankard, gulped, choked and coughed. "Whoa, that's strong."

Adam sat beside her on his bed. "It is not one of your fancy daiquiris."

Diana giggled as she ventured to take another sip.

"You need a strong draft to ward off the cold." He rubbed her shoulders through the robe she'd been wrapped in after her bath. "The hot bath was helpful, but it may not have warmed you throughout."

"Trust me, Adam. I'm warm all over."

"Now, perhaps. But not very long ago, you stood on the precipice. By thunder, if ever anything could have taken ten years from my life, it was the sight of you standing there, only inches from your death."

"I wasn't trying to kill myself. I only wanted to go home," she explained once more. "I'm not the suicidal type, for heaven's sake. Although I guess it did look a little strange—"

"Strange?" Adam shot back at her. "Strange to come home to a wailing Mathilde—"

"I'm sorry, Adam."

"She was crying that you had gone to the bluff to throw yourself in the sea because I had threatened to whip Russell."

"Mathilde tends to get a little confused. You know why I was there, Adam. I went to the bluff so I could be transported back home."

Adam didn't pretend to understand her logic.

"I know—it seems ridiculous. But lightning brought me here, and I thought it could take me back."

Adam sank onto the bed beside her and touched her cheek in that wonderfully familiar way.

"No, Diana, I brought you to Rogue's Cay on the *Black Hawke*."

Diana sighed and took another drink. There was no use getting into that old discussion.

"Diana," Adam said softly, "I had great hope that you would consider this your home now."

"Rogue's Cay my home? How can you say that, when you've made your purpose clear from the first? You're holding me here until it's time to trade me for your father. There's no home for me on Rogue's Cay."

Adam took the tankard from her hand and placed it on the table. Then he slipped his arm around Diana's waist and drew her close. She made an effort to pull away, but he held tightly.

"I'm trying to be angry with you," she said.

Adam laughed.

"It's not funny."

"One is either angry or not angry," Adam told her.

"Then I'm angry. Because of the way you treated Russell. That's why I went out in the storm. I wanted to get away from all that and go home."

"And you were right."

She looked up at him quizzically.

"Not in your desire to leave here, but in your notions about Russell. He is no longer in jail. I understand all."

"Great. Then how about explaining it to me?"

"La Perla had a plan to kidnap you and trade you to Grenville—not for my father, but for gold," he said.

"And Russell?"

"He found out, but before he could come to me, she realized her only choice was to accuse him. The word spread quickly, and for a moment I believed it."

"Such a ridiculous story to make you go off half-cocked...."

His words were low and muffled against her hair as he held on to her. "Because of you."

"Of me?"

"Yes. The scheme never would have worked. But in the process, you could have been harmed."

Diana swallowed hard. Her fate at the hands of La Perla wasn't pleasant to contemplate. "Maybe La Perla would have hurt me, but Russell—never! And you were threatening to beat him," she accused.

"I was wild with anger, but I only wanted to frighten him into confessing what he knew of the plot. I never would have whipped Russell. He has forgiven me. Diana, say you forgive me, too."

Relief flooded through her. "I do, Adam, but the way you acted . . . like a madman."

Once more he spoke softly against her hair. "I was half mad because I am in love, and love makes fools of us all."

Diana wasn't sure she'd heard correctly. "Repeat that, please."

"I am a fool—"

"No, not that part. The part about being in love." Her heart raced wildly, just as it had done when she'd stood in the pouring rain and riotous wind.

"I am in love with you, and the thought that someone might take you from me—I could not bear it, Diana. I love you far too much."

"You love me," Diana spoke in wonder. "You love me."

"How could I not, when you are the most fascinating, contrary, difficult, sensual—"

"You love me!"

They held each other closely, clinging in excitement and pure delight.

The feeling of euphoria that engulfed Diana lasted only until her mind came alive again. "But you're planning to give me away to the man who's supposed to be my godfather, someone I've never even met—"

"No," Adam said. "That will never happen."

"But you have no choice if you're to see your father again."

Adam held her, silently.

"Oh, Adam, you love your father, and you vowed to free him."

"I know." Adam's face was stern. "I will find another way to set him free and keep you safe. I cannot let you go, Diana. Not now, not ever."

Adam leaned over and kissed her. Diana dropped back onto the pillows and let herself flow into the kiss. Against all odds, they'd fallen in love with each other. But did he even know her feelings? Diana started to sit up, but he pushed her gently back and kissed her again, a long, thorough kiss that sent tingles to the tips of her toes.

"I have to tell you something," she whispered against his mouth.

He sighed and sat back, pulling her into his arms. "Then tell me, milady, so that we can get on with our night of love."

"I feel the same way."

"What does this mean?" he asked jokingly.

"It means that I . . . love you."

He kissed her again, powerfully, but Diana was determined to finish her declaration. "I knew that day at the beach, but I didn't say anything because it all seemed so impossible. I thought you were going to send me away to Sir Winston, and I—"

There was laughter in his voice. "You talk far too much, Lady Diana Tremont. I am a man of action, remember."

She slipped her hand inside his heavy damask robe. "Aye, aye, Captain. I remember well."

10

"'Tis not manly to serve a woman."

Diana, propped up against her pillows, smiled. "I think 'tis very manly. After all, 'tis only a little midnight repast."

Adam smiled. "Ah, 'tis good to hear you speak the king's English for a change.

"I thank you, kind sir." She nodded regally. "As for the feast, if you recall, 'twas your idea."

He plopped a laden tray on the bedside table. "I merely mentioned that I had an appetite. You were the one who suggested that I fetch our vittles from the kitchen."

Diana chose a biscuit from the tray and smeared it with jam. "Come sit beside me." She made room on the bed, offered him a bit of her biscuit and then kissed him soundly. "Have I told you recently that I love you?"

"Not in the past ten minutes."

"I love you, Adam."

"I am very grateful for that love."

Diana felt the sting of tears in her eyes. "And I'm grateful to you for protecting me—and for listening.

A lesser man would have locked me in the attic or sent me to the loony bin."

"Explain." This was Adam's new way of responding to her language.

"Crazy house. You know—Bedlam."

He nodded. "The lunatic asylum in London. I know, but I do not believe you mad, not anymore. Just eccentric and imaginative—and very clever. Those words you spoke to me about trial by jury and innocent until proved guilty made me stop and think about my behavior toward Russell. Because of your words, I had much to cogitate on."

"Then I must tell you that those weren't my words. They came from the Bill of Rights, which won't be written until the end of the century—your century. The Bill of Rights changed the history of the United States...I mean the colonies," she said, correcting herself quickly.

Adam took Diana's hand and looked at her thoughtfully. "More messages from the future?"

She nodded.

"This insistence that you come to me from another time is more than I can fathom. Yet your story never changes—" he said.

"Because it's true that I come from another time, and it's possible that I may go back to that time—"

"And leave me, which you tried once to do."

"That was before I understood you, before we understood each other. I wouldn't do such a thing now. But if I had no control over being sent here, do you think I will have control over going back?"

Adam turned her hand in his and raised it to his lips, kissing the palm. "Perhaps no more control than I have over loving you." He raised a dark eyebrow. "Is there a lover waiting for you in this twentieth century?"

Diana burst into laughter. "There is, but he's you!"

"Diana," he said warningly.

"I know, I've told you this before, but when I woke up on the *Black Hawke*, I really believed you were that other Adam Hawke, the man I'd been so instantly drawn to."

"Did you love this man?" There was a hint of jealousy in Adam's voice.

"No, but I had the feeling that if we'd had time together... but we didn't." She gave Adam a lingering kiss. "What you need to understand is that every man I've ever dreamed of has been *you*, whether that man was in my fantasies, aboard the *Swan* or on Rogue's Cay."

"If ever anything was pleasing to me, it is hearing those words. If I am the man in all your dreams, then all is well."

"All is well," she affirmed. "And tomorrow will be a bright new day."

Outside the storm had passed, and thunder was only a distant rumble moving out to sea. "Except tomorrow brings us closer and closer to the time...to the time I'll be traded to Grenville for your father."

Adam pulled her close. "Do not worry, my darling. I am devising a plan that will keep you with me while guaranteeing my father's safe return. It will be resolved in less than a fortnight if all goes well."

Diana shivered. "It had better go well! I have no intention of sailing off with Sir Winston Grenville instead of staying here with you."

"Nothing is nearer to my heart than keeping you with me. It is where you shall remain...forever."

Diana let him hold her close but didn't respond to his words. Adam's "forever" could end in the twinkling of an eye or the flash of lightning. She could be with him on Rogue's Cay for years—or days. There was no way of knowing.

Diana snuggled even closer, taking comfort in the warmth of his body, where she felt safe and secure. "I don't want to think of forever," she admitted. "Let's just think of tonight."

"I like the sound of that, woman." He kissed her and then untangled himself from her arms and swung his feet onto the floor.

"Where're you going?"

"To fetch something for you." He left the circle of lamplight and reappeared a moment later, his hand clenched into a fist.

"A present? Oh, let me see—"

"Do not be greedy, Diana." He sat beside her, his hand still closed tight. "I bought this for you today, to thank you for your honest words about Russell. You are never afraid to speak the truth to me, as painful as that truth may be. You make me look deep inside myself to the darkness buried there."

Diana fought a lump in her throat. Adam's honesty was as precious to her as a love sonnet. "Then you can't be a true barbarian because a barbarian wouldn't have such feelings," she said in an attempt to lighten the mood.

He was still serious. "Russell is free because of you, and I now see the world differently, also because of you. You have changed me—and my heart."

She touched his cheek with her fingertips. "My life is also complete because of you." She smiled. "Knowing you has been quite an adventure."

"An adventure that is only beginning." He opened his fingers to reveal a beautiful ring in the palm of his hand. The ruby stone was set in gold, circled with diamonds.

"Oh, Adam," she breathed, "it's gorgeous."

"I bought it for you in thanks, but to say the truth, I give it in a pledge of my undying love. Will you accept this ring and my love, Diana?"

"Yes, oh, yes." Her hand shook as he slipped the ring on her finger.

"I shall love you forever, my Diana. I have never spoken those words to a woman before, and I never shall again."

Diana blinked away the blinding tears. "I'll never stop loving you, Adam. Across time and through the years—no matter what happens to us...."

He took her in his arms. "Do not cry, my lady. This is no time for tears. It is a time for joy. We have found each other and fallen in love. Even if you are from another time and place, then I must love you twice as much to keep you here beside me."

"You're starting to believe me, aren't you?"

"Perhaps I am. Perhaps it could be possible that our love is so great it transcends time."

"Could it be?"

"I do not know, Diana. Nor do you. But this much I do know. No matter where or when—in your century or my own—we will be together. Do you believe this, Diana?"

"With all my heart, my darling Adam, with all my heart."

TOO SOON those promises were put to the test as Diana found herself in the bow of the *Black Hawke*, awaiting her fate.

The pale morning sky was an ominous shade of yellow beneath brooding gray clouds. Sheet lightning lit up the Atlantic, flashing without accompanying thunder.

She didn't like it. She wouldn't have liked it under any circumstances, but the eerie remembrances of a stormy Cape Canaveral made her even more nervous. Especially since the *Black Hawke* lay at anchor in a cove off the coast of Florida.

It wasn't the Florida she knew. There were no high rises, no condos, no swarms of tourists sunning themselves on the beach. There was only the sea and the sand and a seemingly impenetrable jungle of palm and palmetto trees.

"It will not be long now. My lookouts have noticed their sails."

Diana turned toward Adam. He stood beside her at the rail, tall, strong and handsome in his buccaneer clothes, the pirate of her fantasy, and yet he was her pirate, her lover and her love. There was no trace of anxiety on his face, even though her own heart was racing and a nervous tightening had begun in her throat. She gripped the rail so tightly that her knuckles had turned white.

Adam must have noticed, but he chose to be stalwart—for her sake, Diana knew. He continued in a calm voice.

"They will be coming in on a sloop with a shallow draft. She will be quick and light. The *Black Hawke* is faster, though. Do not worry." He slipped a comforting arm around her waist.

"But I am worried. I'm scared to death."

"There is nothing to fear, Diana."

"Of course there is! I'm afraid of Sir Winston, afraid I won't see you again, afraid—"

"No, my darling, you have no need to fear. I have a plan, and by heaven I will see it through. That much I vow."

"Then please let me know what it is, Adam." Diana couldn't control the trembling in her voice. She lacked Adam's courage.

"I would tell you if it would help our cause, but you would only worry." He wrapped his arm around her shoulder. "When the time comes, you will know all. Promise me that you will do as I tell you and pay no heed to anyone else."

Diana nodded in agreement but after a thoughtful moment had another idea. "Adam, why don't I just explain everything to Sir Winston?"

"Diana—"

"No, I could simply tell him that I'm not the Lady Diana he's expecting—"

"This is not a tea party," Adam responded dryly. "I doubt if Grenville will want to hear your stories."

"But what if I say that I want to stay with you. We can just call off the feud."

Adam shook his head and answered her gently. "Those are mad notions, my love, and he would pay no heed to them."

"But—"

"No, Diana. This peer of the British empire is not going to believe that Lady Diana Tremont, reared in luxury, would choose to stay with a rogue privateer of her own free will. You must know that he would suspect a trick."

Diana's shoulders sagged. "You're probably right. It all sounds too fantastic to be true."

Adam hugged her close. "But it will be over soon, my love. Then, I own, we will be together."

Diana clung to him. His clean, crisp white shirt smelled of sunshine, his skin of the salty sea. The brass buckle of his belt pressed against her, leaving its imprint. She grasped his belt and held on to him with a grip that was like iron, hoping it would keep them together.

But she knew better. "No matter what happens, you'll always be in my heart," she told him. "You know that, don't you?"

He squeezed her in response.

"Even if we're apart physically, we'll never be apart in spirit." Her words sounded desperate even to her own ears. She held on to the belt even more tightly, trying to shake off the terrible sense of foreboding.

Adam leaned down and kissed her. She felt the prickle of his whiskers against her face. It was so real that it gave her courage. He was here with her. He wasn't a phantom. They would be together!

"Yes, we will be together. We will grow old together and see our children and grandchildren come of age. Trust me, Diana."

"I want to believe, Adam."

He continued to hold her close. "It will all go well. Grenville's ship will lower its sails. My men will draw it alongside with grappling hooks and then the negotiations will begin."

"Your father will come aboard the *Black Hawke*, and I—oh, Adam, what will happen to me?"

"Nothing, my love. Do you think I would let harm come to you? Stay alert, and follow my lead. I will not let you go, no matter what transpires."

EVERYTHING HAPPENED as Adam had told her it would. Sir Winston's sloop, the *Good Queen*, lowered her sails and silently, menacingly glided into the cove.

Adam's crew used the wicked-looking grappling hooks to draw the two ships close together. Diana steadied herself against the mast, hidden from view but able to watch from behind the furled sails. The vessels bumped and bobbed in the water. The tide was turning, and waves in the cove slapped at the hull of their vessel.

One man stood out aboard the *Good Queen*. He was finely arrayed in white silk stockings, buckled boots, turquoise satin breeches and red brocade vest, with a tricorn hat perched upon his flowing wig. His coat was shot with threads of gold, and he looked every inch the aristocratic nobleman. She recognized him instantly as Sir Winston Grenville—and she disliked him on sight.

Sir Winston called across the water, "Hawke, show me my goddaughter." His voice was high and nasal and echoed over the open water.

Diana didn't budge from the hiding place where she'd positioned herself.

Adam nodded at her with a silent command to stay where she was. "Not until I see my father, Grenville," he called out.

Grenville nodded as if he'd been expecting the demand. "Bring out the old man," he admonished a crew member.

A hatch was opened. Simon Hawke shuffled up into the sunlight, squinting. Peering around the mast, Diana put her hands to her mouth to stifle an exclamation of dismay. The man who appeared on the deck was pale and thin, dressed in rags, his beard and hair scraggly. Irons encircled his neck and legs, and he walked in shuffling steps.

The old man reached the rail and stood beside Grenville, blinking in the flashing white light that brightened the sky.

Diana looked toward Adam. His face looked carved in stone. "Show yourself, Diana," he said.

Legs shaking, Diana stepped out from her hiding place.

"Thank God you are safe, my child," Grenville called out.

Adam stood silently, and Diana also remained silent, as Adam had instructed.

Just seeing her seemed to be enough to satisfy Grenville. "You have no idea the worries I've suffered. Now if you'll come aboard . . ."

"My father first, Grenville."

"Not on your life, Hawke."

Across the water, the two men glowered at each other. There was no sound except for the creaking of the ships and the shuffling among the crews.

Diana stood beside Adam, praying that Sir Winston would do as Adam had said. Her anxiety was at the explosion level. Whatever was going to happen, she wanted it to happen now. It was time for the scenario to unfold. "For heaven's sake, let's get on with it," she called out, unable to restrain herself.

Sir Winston's mouth dropped open at Diana's words, but he didn't seem to doubt her identity. Finally he managed to make a faint gesture with his hand. At the command, a guard gave Simon Hawke a push, and the old man shuffled forward to the rail.

The ships rubbed together, creaking eerily, parted and then touched again. At that point, two of Adam's burliest sailors grabbed Simon and dragged him over onto the *Black Hawke*, where he collapsed onto the deck, muttering incoherently.

Adam took a step toward the old man, who'd allowed himself to be lifted by the sailors. Their eyes met, and the look of love and understanding that passed between them was powerful and moving.

Grenville couldn't have noticed, so fleeting was the exchange. Then Adam stepped back, assumed his earlier posture, and ordered, "Get my father below." With that he returned his gaze to the foppish figure still standing at the rail of the *Good Queen*.

"We will trade the lady next, Grenville."

Diana looked sharply at Adam. There was no reassurance in his cold and implacable voice. She knew it must be a part of his plan, and yet it turned her blood cold. She didn't feel any better when he grabbed her upper arm and led her to the rail.

"Come forward and claim the wench, Grenville. From my hands to yours, just as we agreed."

He gave her a little push.

Diana turned and looked back at Adam, hoping to see in his eyes a fleeting look of love like the one he'd turned upon his father. But there was nothing.

"I will hand her over to you and no one else," Adam called out.

Fear gripped Diana's heart and made her legs weak. What was the matter with Adam? He was acting as if he were really going to trade her! What was going on?

Diana began to resist, but Adam held on more tightly.

"Adam," she murmured.

He leaned down until his lips touched her ear. "When I say now, grab that wretched peacock's vest and hold on for all you are worth. Do you understand?"

Diana made a sound that she hoped was affirmative. Her heart pounded so loudly she was sure that Sir Winston as well as Adam could hear it.

Adam stopped at the *Black Hawke*'s railing. "Come and claim your prize, Grenville. You are welcome to her." He held Diana out in front of him.

Mesmerized, she watched her "godfather" come toward them. Behind him she could see his crewmen raise their muskets. She sensed that Adam's men were doing the same. She prayed softly to herself, "Please make this work. Make it end soon."

The sky still glowed with eerie silent lightning. The whole horizon seemed lit with its yellow cast.

Grenville approached, wary and yet obviously relieved to have her so close at last. She dared not speak for fear her voice would give it all away, but she offered herself, taking a deep breath and stretching her arms toward him.

He leaned forward, smiling triumphantly. That's when Adam shouted. "Now, Diana!"

Diana grabbed the lapels of Grenville's frock and held on with all her might. The *Black Hawke creaked mightily, then shifted with the subtle, but steady, running of the tide, and threw them both off balance. Grenville teetered toward the Black Hawke* and fell forward onto Diana.

Russell was there to catch her and pull her backward. But she still held on to Grenville's lapels for dear life.

"Release him," Russell cried. "For God's sake, let the man go."

Diana dropped her hands, and Adam heaved Grenville onto the *Black Hawke.*

"Raise the sails, mates," he shouted, "and race for the Keys. We will leave Grenville there and then... home!"

There was panic and confusion aboard the *Good Queen.* Men brandished muskets but were afraid to fire with Sir Winston blocking Adam.

As the crewmen scurried to raise the sails, suddenly from nowhere the thunder roared, the wind shifted and the seas betrayed them. One mighty roll of the ship threw Adam off balance.

In the instant that Adam fought to regain his footing, Grenville was free, shouting hysterically to his crew. "Fire, you bloody fools. You have a clear shot. Fire!"

From the other ship, Diana saw a lone crewman find Adam in his sights. Without thinking, she drove her elbow into Russell's ribs and broke loose, her adrenaline pumping as she hurled herself across the deck.

As she moved, the heavens seemed to break open with a blinding flash of light and a great roar of thunder. Or was it the sound of the musket and the flash of its shot?

She didn't stop to wonder as she threw her body between the death-dealing shot and Adam, its target. She felt a warmth go through her and everything exploded in a blaze of white light.

"OH, PLEASE get the light out of my eyes," Diana cried. She twisted and turned, but the blinding, penetrating light persisted.

"So, you're awake. Welcome back, Ms. Tremont."

The source of bright light was turned away. Diana blinked once, squinted and then focused. A man dressed in white leaned over her, a penlight in his hand.

"Who are you?" Diana managed. "Where's Adam?"

"I'm Dr. Webb, and you're a patient at Orlando Medical Center. I don't know where Adam is—or who he is."

"Adam Hawke, of course," Diana told him with irritation. "Captain of the *Black Hawke*."

Dr. Webb shook his head uninterestedly.

"I was with him on the ship—" Suddenly the doctor's words penetrated the fuzziness in her head. "Orlando? I'm back in Orlando?"

"That's right." The young doctor busied himself taking her pulse, a frown of concentration on his otherwise baby-smooth face.

"How long have I been here?"

"Three days. Since New Year's Eve." The doctor pocketed the light and made careful notes on his chart.

"That's not possible. I was on Rogue's Cay for weeks!" Diana struggled to sit up.

Dr. Webb smiled patronizingly. "Confusion after a coma is quite common, Ms. Tremont, but in another twenty-four hours you'll be fine." He returned her chart to the foot of the bed and crossed to the door. "We're going to remove your IVs and get you on solid food. You'll be out of here in no time."

Before she could respond he added, "I'll send in your nurse."

Diana sank back on her pillow. A coma—she'd been in a coma! No, that couldn't be possible. Could it? Could Adam Hawke, Rogue's Cay, Russell, Mathilde and La Perla have all been a dream? She closed her eyes and tried to think clearly. Two ships anchored off the coast . . . the exchange . . . the gun-fire . . . the thunder . . . and finally a blinding light.

Was it possible that none of it had happened, that she'd been lying comatose in a hospital bed all that time? Could Adam have existed only in her dreams? Overcome by a terrible sense of loss, Diana turned toward the wall and let the tears flow.

THE NEXT MORNING, Mindy bounded into the hospital room carrying a huge bouquet of flowers and a box of candy.

"Here I am! I saw your parents in the hall, and they said you're almost ready to go home. What a relief! We were all so worried, but you look great!"

"I feel fine. A little tired and sometimes confused—" Very confused, Diana thought to herself.

"That's understandable." Mindy bustled around and found a vase for the flowers. "They're from Harry. The candy's from me. You probably guessed that "

"Thanks, Mindy."

"There're a lot of flowers here...." Mindy poked through the cards. "Aha, I thought so—this bouquet's from Adam Hawke."

Adam Hawke. Yes, Diana thought. But not the Adam Hawke to whom she'd sworn her undying love. Once more the tears formed. This time she blinked them back.

"Where is he now?" Diana wondered aloud.

"Off on a flight somewhere." Mindy was talking about the other Adam. "He didn't have to be hospitalized, but believe me, he's been here a lot. He's called Harry and me a zillion times."

"Slow down. Let's take it from the top. How did I get here? The last thing I remember was a tree limb falling toward me."

"Did you see your life pass by? Did it all go all black like in the movies?"

"Mindy, I'm asking the questions."

"Okay. Here's what Adam told me. The storm was raging all around, and you guys were the only ones on the beach. You broke away from him and ran. A huge tree limb was torn off and fell on you. Then all the lights on the ship went out. Everything was dark."

"I don't remember anything after the crack of lightning."

"No, you were out cold by then. And the branch had you pinned. I guess it took him forever to get you out from all the rubble. There was an emergency phone at the dock, but the lines were down. So he carried you to the car and drove to the hospital. He was probably scared to death that you were going to die, because you were just lying there with your eyes rolled back in your head."

"Mindy, did he tell you that?"

"No, but that's what happens in comas, isn't it?" She didn't wait for a response. "Anyway, I think what he did was real heroic."

"I don't know about that, but it was certainly gallant. He could just have taken me to the ship and hoped an ambulance would get through."

"Not Adam. He's a man of action, and he's really been worried about you."

"I wish I could remember something—anything—about it." Diana pressed her fingertips against her temples. The Adam Hawke who'd rescued her from the storm was confused in her head with Captain

Adam Hawke, her lover. Both were heroic and dashing. Both were men of her fantasies.

"I need to rest awhile," she told Mindy.

"Great, boss. I'll go back to the shop and check in with Harry. Everything's going great so you don't have to worry. You get discharged this afternoon, and I told your folks I'd take you home. There'll probably be more flowers there—and maybe even a surprise or two."

"I can do without any more surprises," Diana replied, closing her eyes so that she missed Mindy's mischievous smile.

DIANA WAS BACK in her own house, stretched out on her white wicker. She was wearing her favorite hot-pink jogging suit, and her hair was still damp from a long soothing bath. From the kitchen came the noise of Mindy clattering pots and cups. Familiar sights and sounds.

Diana sighed deeply. She should have been content. She loved her home, and she vowed to spend more time in it and to concentrate—for a change—on her personal life. No more workaholic compulsiveness. "To live each day to the fullest, just as I did with Adam," she whispered. Adam. How could she be content without him? Delusion or not, she missed him dreadfully. Diana fought against the aching loneliness inside and wondered if she could ever experience joy again.

She'd been over it all a hundred times and decided there were two ways to look at the situation. One was the sensible, obvious, practical way. While in her coma, she'd imagined Rogue's Cay, the piratical Adam Hawke and all the rest.

Then there was the other fanciful, imaginative, crazy possibility. While her physical being was lying in the hospital, stuck with IVs and carefully monitored, another part of her had been on Rogue's Cay in the year 1724, falling in love with Adam Hawke.

Improbable as it seemed, her time with Adam had been too real to be a delusion. She wanted to believe it had happened, but it didn't seem that she'd ever know.

She closed her eyes tightly and willed Adam to send her a sign. All she got was Mindy, bustling into the room with a tray.

"Tea and toast, jam, cake and cookies. Everyone's had a hand in stocking your refrigerator."

Mindy put the tray on the table by the sofa.

"Aren't you joining me?" Diana asked.

"Well, I guess I could have a cookie." Mindy chose one but didn't sit down, hovering around the window, instead.

"What's the matter with you, Mindy? You seem—"

The slam of a car door sent Mindy into action. "Next shift coming on duty. See you tomorrow, boss." She grabbed her coat and bag and was out the door.

Diana stood up and started to call out, but something stopped her, a sense of excitement that quickened her heartbeat and shortened her breath. It could have been her mother or father, any one of her friends. Yet something told her it was none of them. Something told her it was Adam.

He appeared in the hallway. He was as tall as she remembered, and just as handsome. His dark wavy hair was brushed back from his face. He wore a leather bomber jacket, blue shirt, khaki pants. They were modern clothes, but that didn't matter. It was Adam. The rakish smile was the same, as were the tilt of his head, the breadth of his shoulders.

The shock of seeing him had rooted Diana to the spot, but he moved quickly, crossing the room in two strides to take her in his arms.

"I need to hold you and hug you and see for myself that you're all right."

"How..." She tried to form a question.

"I told Mindy I'd be here as soon as my plane touched down. Didn't she tell you? Are you all right?" His eyes were dark with concern.

"I'm fine. Really." Diana hugged him back. He felt solid...and very real, just as she'd remembered. "I'm a little confused, that's all."

"No wonder, after what you've been through." He reached out and touched her cheek with his fingertips, that old familiar touch that was so much like Adam. *Her* Adam. Diana felt the blood rush to her face and her heart hammer wildly.

"I need to thank you." She tried to quell the quiver in her voice.

"Thank me?" With one arm tightly around her, Adam led Diana to the sofa and sat beside her.

"You were a hero. You rescued me."

Adam laughed, a sound as familiar as his touch. "I was there, that's all."

"Lucky for me."

"What a first date, huh?"

"It was a little unusual." She couldn't help staring at him. He was so much like the Adam she'd known on Rogue's Cay, yet he wasn't that Adam. Or was he? Had she created that Adam because of *this* Adam?

"Is something the matter, Diana?"

"I'm sorry. It's just that...that I was thinking of how we met."

"That was the luckiest night of my life. I told you then, but you probably thought it was a line. I believe it now. Fate led me to Fantasy Faire."

"That night . . . It seems so long ago."

Adam shrugged. "Time is relative, Diana. I fly from one time zone to another, but that doesn't change me. I'm on my own personal time."

"I've been wondering about time...and travel...a lot lately." She didn't say "time travel," even though that's what she was thinking.

"You'll figure it out," he said, looking at her intently.

His eyes were so familiar, dark brown with flecks of green and gold, and Diana felt drawn into them. The feeling was almost magical, and she wondered if Adam felt it, too.

He took her hand. "I had to be with you today, Diana. Maybe it's presumptuous of me, but I wanted to be here when you came home. We've been through so much together."

If he only knew how much, Diana thought as she squeezed his hand.

Adam took that as encouragement to go on. "I've thought about you constantly since the night of the gala. Flying over the ocean at night, I'd see your face in the stars. Waking up in a strange hotel, I'd think of you and wish you were with me. I even imagined you with me. Isn't that weird? It's never happened to me before."

"No, it's not weird at all," Diana said. "It's quite wonderful, really, that you thought about me the whole time I was in the hospital."

"The whole time," he repeated. "I have proof that you were on my mind. Just a minute." He brought in his flight bag from the hallway. "I found a couple of presents for you in the islands." He rummaged in the canvas bag and pulled out a bottle. "I'm taking a chance that you're a woman who likes daiquiris."

She swallowed hard. "I love them."

"Well, this is the best rum you've ever tasted, straight from the Caribbean. When the doctor gives the okay, I'll mix us a batch of frozen daiquiris that will be out of this world." He laughed. "Actually, they're easy to make. A little rum, lime juice—"

"And sugar," she ventured. Those were the same words she'd said to Adam on Rogue's Cay. It probably meant nothing. Plenty of people liked daiquiris and knew the recipe. Still, she found her heart beating more quickly. There was something expectant in the air.

Again Adam rummaged in his flight bag and this time came up with a package wrapped in brown paper.

Diana took it eagerly, and her hands shook when she ripped at the paper.

Adam stopped her. "First, let me tell you how I found it." He sat beside her. "My last stop was on a little island called Rogue's Cay."

Diana felt her heart race.

"I think I mentioned it before."

She nodded mutely.

"I went exploring, and I stumbled on an old house way up on a bluff. It's been turned into an inn and antique shop, done up for tourists, of course. There's even a legend about its once being a pirate's hang-out."

Diana tried to catch her breath and found herself gasping.

"Are you okay?"

"Fine," she managed.

"They sell curios and souvenirs at the shop and now and then something rare. What I picked up was a real find, stuck on a shelf behind some old curios."

There was a roaring in her ears. She knew what was inside! With trembling hands, Diana opened the package. The leather binding was cracked and broken, the pages yellowed and brittle with age. "Robinson Crusoe," she murmured. "Seventeen-nineteen."

Her heart was so full of hope that she felt it might burst. She couldn't stop the tears that welled and began to course down her cheeks. She wiped them away with the back of her hand.

Adam looked concerned. "Diana, are you all right? I didn't mean to upset you."

"Upset me? No, I'm not upset. This is fantastic. Oh, you don't know *how* fantastic!" All the wonder of the day came back to her. This must be a sign.

"I hope it's authentic."

Diana opened the book. It *seemed* to be her book from Rogue's Cay, but how could she be sure? She flipped to the front and then to the back. No sketch.

There'd been nothing memorable about the book. Only the sketch she'd drawn. And it was gone.

She'd thought it was a sign, the sign she'd been waiting for, but now she wasn't sure. Maybe it was only a coincidence that Adam had brought the book to her.

He didn't seem to notice her pensive look as he ran his fingers across the old leather. "It was written so long ago, but that's part of the fascination, isn't it? Time is relative. For you and me, this book is now. *We're* now. I'd like to think that you and I were fated somehow to be together," he mused. "I know that sounds overly romantic and men aren't supposed to be romantic." He touched her cheek and let his hand wander down her neck.

The gesture was so familiar and seductive that Diana gave in to it. "Men should always be romantic," she whispered. "But I think we've had enough talk." She grew suddenly bold. "Kiss me, Adam." For a moment she forgot all about signs from the past.

"With pleasure."

His mouth was hot and sweet, hungry for hers. He cupped her head with one hand and drew her even closer. Diana gave a little moan of pleasure, and the kiss deepened. His tongue touched hers. She caressed the soft skin at the back of his neck, the crisp texture of his hair, the hard muscles of his back.

He was Adam, her Adam. They clung to each other, heart beating against heart. Diana sighed. His body was warm and strong and familiar. A joyous feeling washed over her. It was like coming in from the dark to a warm sunlit room. Being in his arms felt so right, so very, very right. She was safe and complete.

And yet she'd never really received the sign she so wanted. If only there were some proof that they'd been together centuries ago.

"I wanted to kiss you like that from the first minute I saw you," Adam murmured. He nuzzled her behind the ear. "I wanted to grab you and kiss you and hold you. That would have been a little ridiculous in your shop, but that's what I wanted." He kissed her again and then moved away, holding her at arms length, looking at her deeply, he asked "Am I going too fast for you?"

"Time is relative, Adam," she answered.

He kissed her again, tender nibbling kisses along her upper lip, her cheek, her chin. She felt as though she were floating in tepid water, warmed by a tropical sun. Heat flowed through her veins and warmed her to the center of her being.

"There's one more thing," Adam whispered against her mouth. "Just before I left the hospital, the nurse gave this to me." He rummaged in his pocket. "It's your ring."

"Ring? I wore earrings that night, a necklace and a headpiece with feathers and tulle, but no other jewelry. Certainly not a ring." Diana was curious as Adam sat up and pulled an envelope from his pocket.

"Well, they seemed certain this belonged to you. Hold out your hand." He opened the envelope and put the ring in her hand. It was a ruby surrounded by diamonds. The ring Adam had given her!

Diana felt as though her heart would burst with happiness. She closed her eyes and grasped the ring in her hand until the cold hard stone bit into her flesh. It was real—not a delusion, not a coma-induced hallucination, but real!

Diana needed no more reassurance. She knew for certain that for a while she'd lived in another time and loved a pirate named Adam Hawke. He'd given her the ring as a token of their love. Now fate was giving her another chance to love that man once more.

And love him she would!

She opened her eyes and smiled into the eyes of the man who was her fantasy—and her one true love.

A slight frown crossed his forehead. "The funny thing is, I don't remember you wearing a ring, either."

"There's a lot that you don't know."

He wrapped her in his arms again. "Well," he whispered against her hair, "I want to know everything about you, Diana Tremont. I'm hoping to spend a lot of time with you."

"I'm so glad, Adam. I made a promise to myself, a vow to let my personal life come first for a change. You're definitely in my personal life."

"Thank heavens for that—and for costume shops—"

"And pirate outfits and the wonderful man who stepped into the shop and into a woman's fantasies." She kissed him slowly, lingeringly. "Can you stay with me a while tonight?"

"All night, if you'll let me," he answered. "And tomorrow and the next day. Oh, Diana," he murmured between kisses, "I've wanted to spend the night with you since the first moment we met."

Diana sighed, a sound of satisfaction and completion.

"Good, because I have a story to tell you."

He held her close. "I can't wait to hear it."

"It might take a long time," she said.

"Time is relative, Diana."

She smiled and raised her lips to his.

Earth, Wind, Fire, Water
The four elements—but nothing is
more elemental than passion.

Join us for *Passion's Quest,* four sizzling, action-packed
romances in the tradition of *Romancing the Stone* and
The African Queen. Starting in January 1994, one book each
month is a sexy, romantic adventure focusing on the quest
for passion...set against the essential elements of earth,
wind, fire and water.

On sale in February
To banish the February blahs, there's *Wild Like the Wind* by
Janice Kaiser. When her vengeful ex-husband kidnapped her
beloved daughter Zara, Julia Powell hired Cole Bonner to
rescue her. She was depending on the notorious mercenary's
strength and stealth to free her daughter. What she hadn't
counted on was the devastating effect of this wild and
passionate man on *her.*

The quest continues...
Coming in March—*Aftershock* by Lynn Michaels
And in April—*Undercurrent* by Lisa Harris.

Passion's Quest—four fantastic adventures,
four fantastic love stories

AVAILABLE NOW: *Body Heat* by Elise Title (#473)

Take 4 bestselling love stories FREE

Plus get a FREE surprise gift!

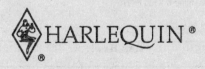

NEW YORK TIMES Bestselling Author

Barbara DELINSKY

returns in January with

The Real Thing

Stranded on an island off the coast of Maine,
Deirdre Joyce and Neil Hersey got the
solitude they so desperately craved—
but they also got each other, something they
hadn't expected. Nor had they expected
to be consumed by a desire so powerful
that the idea of living alone again was
unimaginable. A marrige of "convenience"
made sense—or did it? B087

 HARLEQUIN®

HARLEQUIN®

Temptation®

If you missed any Lovers & Legends titles, here's your chance to order them:

Harlequin Temptation®—*Lovers & Legends*

#425	THE PERFECT HUSBAND by Kristine Rolofson	$2.99	☐
#433	THE MISSING HEIR by Leandra Logan	$2.99	☐
#437	DR. HUNK by Glenda Sanders	$2.99	☐
#441	THE VIRGIN AND THE UNICORN by Kelly Street	$2.99	☐
#445	WHEN IT'S RIGHT by Gina Wilkins	$2.99	☐
#449	SECOND SIGHT by Lynn Michaels	$2.99	☐
#453	THE PRINCE AND THE SHOWGIRL by JoAnn Ross	$2.99	☐
#457	YOU GO TO MY HEAD by Bobby Hutchinson	$2.99	☐
#461	NIGHT WATCH by Carla Neggers	$2.99	☐
#465	NAUGHTY TALK by Tiffany White	$2.99	☐
#469	I'LL BE SEEING YOU by Kristine Rolofson	$2.99	☐

(limited quantities available on certain titles)

TOTAL AMOUNT	$
POSTAGE & HANDLING	$
($1.00 for one book, 50¢ for each additional)	
APPLICABLE TAXES*	$
TOTAL PAYABLE	$ _____
(check or money order—please do not send cash)	_____

To order, complete this form and send it, along with a check or money order for the total above, payable to Harlequin Books, to: *In the U.S.*: 3010 Walden Avenue, P.O. Box 9047, Buffalo, NY 14269-9047; *In Canada*: P.O. Box 613, Fort Erie, Ontario, L2A 5X3.

Name: _____

Address: _____ City: _____

State/Prov.: _____ Zip/Postal Code: _____

*New York residents remit applicable sales taxes.
 Canadian residents remit applicable GST and provincial taxes.

LLF

Fifty red-blooded, white-hot, true-blue hunks
from every State in the Union!

Look for MEN MADE IN AMERICA! Written by some
of our most poplar authors, these stories feature fifty of
the strongest, sexiest men, each from a different state in
the union!

Two titles available every other month at your favorite
retail outlet.

In January, look for:

DREAM COME TRUE by Ann Major (Florida)
WAY OF THE WILLOW by Linda Shaw (Georgia)

In March, look for:

TANGLED LIES by Anne Stuart (Hawaii)
ROGUE'S VALLEY by Kathleen Creighton (Idaho)

You won't be able to resist MEN MADE IN AMERICA!

HARLEQUIN®

Don't miss these Harlequin favorites by some of our most distinguished authors!
And now, you can receive a discount by ordering two or more titles!

HT#25409	THE NIGHT IN SHINING ARMOR by JoAnn Ross	$2.99	☐
HT#25471	LOVESTORM by JoAnn Ross	$2.99	☐
HP#11463	THE WEDDING by Emma Darcy	$2.89	☐
HP#11592	THE LAST GRAND PASSION by Emma Darcy	$2.99	☐
HR#03188	DOUBLY DELICIOUS by Emma Goldrick	$2.89	☐
HR#03248	SAFE IN MY HEART by Leigh Michaels	$2.89	☐
HS#70464	CHILDREN OF THE HEART by Sally Garrett	$3.25	☐
HS#70524	STRING OF MIRACLES by Sally Garrett	$3.39	☐
HS#70500	THE SILENCE OF MIDNIGHT by Karen Young	$3.39	☐
HI#22178	SCHOOL FOR SPIES by Vickie York	$2.79	☐
HI#22212	D'ANGEROUS VINTAGE by Laura Pender	$2.89	☐
HI#22219	TORCH JOB by Patricia Rosemoor	$2.89	☐
HAR#16459	MACKENZIE'S BABY by Anne McAllister	$3.39	☐
HAR#16466	A COWBOY FOR CHRISTMAS by Anne McAllister	$3.39	☐
HAR#16462	THE PIRATE AND HIS LADY by Margaret St. George	$3.39	☐
HAR#16477	THE LAST REAL MAN by Rebecca Flanders	$3.39	☐
HH#28704	A CORNER OF HEAVEN by Theresa Michaels	$3.99	☐
HH#28707	LIGHT ON THE MOUNTAIN by Maura Seger	$3.99	☐

Harlequin Promotional Titles

#83247	YESTERDAY COMES TOMORROW by Rebecca Flanders	$4.99	☐
#83257	MY VALENTINE 1993	$4.99	☐
	(short-story collection featuring Anne Stuart, Judith Arnold, Anne McAllister, Linda Randall Wisdom)		

(limited quantities available on certain titles)

	AMOUNT	$
DEDUCT:	10% DISCOUNT FOR 2+ BOOKS	$
ADD:	POSTAGE & HANDLING	$
	($1.00 for one book, 50¢ for each additional)	
	APPLICABLE TAXES*	$ _____
	TOTAL PAYABLE	$ _____
	(check or money order—please do not send cash)	

To order, complete this form and send it, along with a check or money order for the total above, payable to Harlequin Books, to: **In the U.S.:** 3010 Walden Avenue, P.O. Box 9047, Buffalo, NY 14269-9047; **In Canada:** P.O. Box 613, Fort Erie, Ontario, L2A 5X3.

Name: _____

Address: _____ City: _____

State/Prov.: _____ Zip/Postal Code: _____

*New York residents remit applicable sales taxes.
Canadian residents remit applicable GST and provincial taxes.

HBACK-JM